His daughter.

There she was.

He could never mistake her for any but his own, though she had Faith's eyes.

"*Mia cara bambina...*"

Words failed him and inside his chest it felt as though someone squeezed his heart in warm hands. His Chloe was taller than he'd expected and more curious than he had hoped for as her little face tilted sideways and she examined him with interest.

He looked back at his daughter. She held out her hand as if she were a five-year-old queen. "*Buongiorno,*" she said with an Australian accent, and he laughed.

"*Buongiorno, piccolo.*" He glanced at Faith and for an instant he saw what she had hidden behind her apparent serenity. The clenched hands of trepidation, the chewed lip of hope that he would be a good father for Chloe, the bowed head of having to share her baby with another parent after all these years.

In a second he saw that and vowed he would protect the mother as well as the child.

Dear Reader,

I hope you enjoy the third installment of The Midwives of Lighthouse Bay. It's so wonderful for me to be back with our lovely midwives and the heroes who deserve them.

This is Faith's story, an inspiring single mom who fell in love once, long ago. When Faith discovered she was pregnant and Raimondo didn't answer her letters, she dedicated herself to being the best mom she could be for her baby. Her midwife friends in Lighthouse Bay surrounded her with love and emotional support, along with her amazing aunt, but almost six years later…

Dr. Raimondo Salvanelli fell in love once, in a far-off land, but flew home to Italy to marry for family duty at the deathbed of his grandfather. Almost six years later, he's divorced and buried in his work, and his friend has just attended a wedding in Lighthouse Bay. This friend mentioned the child of the unmarried woman he'd loved.

What if… Five years old? Surely not, or he would have returned!

This is the story of two people and a child whose happiness is the most important thing to both of them, and also a story about finding lost love. I hope you enjoy Faith and Raimondo's story as much in the reading as I did in the writing.

With warmest regards,

xx *Fi*

FionaMcArthurAuthor.com

THE MIDWIFE'S SECRET CHILD

FIONA McARTHUR

HARLEQUIN® MEDICAL ROMANCE™

ISBN-13: 978-1-335-14914-5

The Midwife's Secret Child

First North American Publication 2019

This edition published by arrangement with Harlequin Books S.A.

For questions and comments about the quality of this book, please contact us at CustomerService@Harlequin.com.

Printed in U.S.A.

Books by Fiona McArthur

Harlequin Medical Romance

The Midwives of Lighthouse Bay

A Month to Marry the Midwife
Healed by the Midwife's Kiss

Christmas in Lyrebird Lake

Midwife's Christmas Proposal
Midwife's Mistletoe Baby

A Doctor, A Fling & A Wedding Ring
The Prince Who Charmed Her
Gold Coast Angels: Two Tiny Heartbeats
Christmas with Her Ex

Visit the Author Profile page
at Harlequin.com for more titles.

To Dianne Latham, who won the name in the book competition, and the Lilli Pilli Ladies of the Macleay Valley, who raise money for those being treated for cancer, toward their comfort, and all the wonderful people who support LPL's fab fundraising days. You rock.

Praise for
Fiona McArthur

"[A] book that was filled with plenty of emotion—both happy and sad, two characters that need each other to heal from their painful pasts and a storyline that illustrates love is worth fighting for."

—*Harlequin Junkie* on
A Month to Marry the Midwife

CHAPTER ONE

Friday

FAITH FETHERSTONE TAPPED her watch as she stood under the meeting point for the Binimirr Underground Complex. Outside in the car park gravel scattered with a late arrival and the vehicle's throaty rumble deepened then silenced as the newcomer pulled in and stopped. The butcher birds, previously revelling in the bush sunshine, ceased their song as a lone cloud passed over the sun and Faith shivered.

The caves kiosk, which held all the caving equipment as well as promoting the cave-themed mementos of the area, straddled the entrance to the labyrinth which stood tucked into the hill ten kilometres south of Lighthouse Bay.

Faith, today's cave guide, tugged down her 'Ultimate Caving Adventure' T-shirt, which clung too tightly, and thought that perhaps her decision to tumble-dry it on hot when she was running late this morning had been less than wise.

She shrugged. It might stretch later and everyone would be looking at the caves not at her. She tucked away the hair that had escaped her ponytail to surreptitiously study the varied group of adults assembled inside the tourist shop, ready for her tour.

Dianne behind the cash register held up one finger. So, one still to arrive; hopefully that had been his car outside. So far her only concern seemed the quiet man in his twenties who chewed his nails and glanced towards the entrance to the caves with an intense frown. She'd watch for symptoms of claustrophobia down in the labyrinth.

The most striking group member at the moment had to be the thin, twinkling-eyed older gentleman in an iridescent orange buttoned shirt and matching shoes, an outfit that Faith thought just might glow in the dark once they turned out the lights.

Barney Burrows, proudly seventy years young, had caved in his youth, and chatted to the short, solid woman in her forties, while her two taller teenage sons conversed with a young backpacker couple.

The backpackers had smiling, animated faces and Eastern European accents but their excellent grasp of English reassured Faith they would understand her if she needed to give instructions fast.

Sudden movement at the door made Faith's head turn, her welcome extinguished like a billy of water dumped on a campfire.

A dark-haired, well-muscled man with his haughty Roman nose angled her way loomed in the doorway. A full-lipped sensuous mouth, a mouth she'd never quite been able to forget, unfortunately, held a definite hint of hardness she'd not noticed the last time.

But that had been a long time ago. Those halcyon days had ended after that cryptic phone call from his family back across the world and had removed him from her side.

This man had sworn he could never, ever come back to Lighthouse Bay. Yet here he was. Returned? The prickle on her skin as his glance captured hers was a heated reminder of a limited infatuation of a few intense days, but mammoth proportions.

Lordy, she'd been naive, about twenty, and he a worldly twenty-eight.

Almost six years ago.

Raimondo Salvanelli, here?

The man who'd orchestrated her personal Shakespearean tragedy and the guilty party who'd exited stage left to return to Italy and instantly marry another woman.

She might regret her infatuation but never, ever the consequences of the ribbon of time that had changed her life.

She'd even fairly rapidly come to terms with Raimondo's inevitable absence, accepting they'd not been destined for happily ever after. Just an Italian doctor who didn't practise as a doctor and an Australian midwife, passing in the night.

Actually, several nights.

He'd said he wasn't coming back.

Um. So why was he here?

Worse, had he brought his Italian wife for the cave tour and she'd be right in behind him? No. She couldn't see that happening. Besides, her boss had only held up one finger.

The slight hysteria in the last thought resolved and Faith lifted her chin.

She looked again—and accepted that her

daughter's father really had arrived and was going to be crawling around behind her in the dark for the next hour or so. Without any premonition on her part or warning on his. Excellent. Not.

To her disgust, she'd never found a man who could hold her attention quite so effortlessly. Apparently, that inevitable fascination was still the same.

An immense man, and harshly handsome, with that mouth she only remembered for its humorous and sexy slant. Now there was grimness—which, unfairly, didn't detract from the picture as much as it should—hence the reason to watch him with the wary fascination she'd have if he were a magnificently coloured red-bellied black snake on a bush path.

Apart from his dark, dark eyes and his way too sexy lips she could see her daughter in him, something she'd always wondered about and a fact that perusal of the newspaper photographs had hidden.

Chloe's dad was here. Holy freakin' cow. And why now?

What did this mean for Chloe? Or Faith?

What made Raimondo present today

when he hadn't responded when she'd written of her pregnancy?

He had been equally silent to her brief note after Chloe's birth. No reply by mail or any form of correspondence. Not even to enquire if they were both well, which had shown a coldness she hadn't predicted.

Well, the silence had been unexpected but understood. Sort of. After that phone call from his brother that had ended everything, Raimondo had announced he'd been going home to marry another woman. Hence the never coming back. Or responding to mail either, apparently.

Yet she'd planned to send another note when Chloe started school next year. And perhaps another when her daughter began her senior years.

She'd fought against allowing his disregard to inflame her because she should still pave the way if Chloe wished to pursue meeting her father in the future.

This had never been about Faith—it was about Chloe.

All about Chloe.

But now he was here. Raimondo's dark eyes travelled slowly over her and, surprisingly, they narrowed, as did his mouth.

Even as the eternal optimist, Faith could see something was wrong.

Well, whatever it was, she knew it wasn't her fault. She lifted her chin higher.

The possible implications of Raimondo revisiting her life opened like an unexpectedly dark flower in front of her and sent a flutter of maternal panic to quicken her breath.

He had rights.

She'd confirmed his claim in letters.

His name on the birth certificate, something she'd considered long and hard, saw to that as well.

She frowned and looked away in out-of-character confusion until accidentally glimpsing Dianne, her caving mentor, her caring friend and also her silver-haired boss, at the counter gesturing to Raimondo and the clock. The tour owner's hands were making exuberant waving motions as she encouraged Faith to commence the tour.

Faith glanced guiltily at the time. Five past ten already. The group peered her way expectantly.

All who had paid, including the man at the door, had arrived and it was time to leave. Good grief. It felt like too much to switch brains to tour guide after the shock-wave of Raimondo's arrival.

Compartments.

Faith could do compartments.

Faith would have to do emergency situation compartments. Navigating herself and other people through life challenges was her bread and butter in her real profession as a midwife and she'd just have to drag that skill across to caving tours with the man she'd thought she'd never see again.

She could do that.

Mentally she clanked shut doors and boxes in her brain like a theme park gate keeper—clang, bolt, lock until all darting terrors were mostly inside... But Raimondo still loomed across the room. The man who was never coming back. And with a scowl as if he'd been the one left holding the baby.

Faith moistened her suddenly dry lips and cleared her throat.

Later. It would have to be later. 'Good morning. My name is Faith.' She remembered the way his soft vowels had caressed her name and, darn it, she could feel the heat on her cheeks but she pushed on and smiled more determinedly. 'I hope you're

all as excited as I am to enjoy the glories of Binimirr Cave this morning.'

Her gaze swept over the others, avoiding the tall, overwhelming presence of the Italian man who'd positioned himself to the back of the group. With a tinge of tour guide unease she hoped his shoulders would fit through one particular narrow opening she could think of in the labyrinth ahead, but reassured herself he'd managed last time. When she'd given him the private tour all those years ago.

Her gaze refocused on the other participants, realised belatedly that the backpackers were in shorts and shook her head. She should have seen that earlier. Every time she crawled through the labyrinth she came home with scratches on her knees and she always wore jeans.

She said gently to everyone, 'This isn't your normal ramble through the paths and steps of a tourist cave. This adventure tour you've signed up for is off the level track and through rough confines. Which means you have to crawl over rough gravel on your knees, squeezing your shoulders and balancing on uneven rocks.'

Faith smiled, admittedly a little blindly,

as her brain batted at her like a bat outside a window trying to comprehend why Raimondo would come back when he'd explained very gently five years ago why he never could or would.

Stop it. Clang. Stay locked.

She rubbed her own elbows and knees. 'Unless you're okay with losing your skin I'm very happy to give you a few minutes to pull some jeans on or buy some knee and elbow guards.'

Most of the participants had arrived on the dusty bus parked outside the shop and the scantily clad young couple peeled off from the group and headed for the tour bus at a fast jog. They were very sweet to be so eager. The quiet, nervous man crossed to the inexpensive knee supports and selected a set to purchase.

From the corner of her eyes she could see Raimondo standing to the back like a dark predator, motionless, an ability she suddenly remembered and had admired then, as others shifted and chatted, and against her will she slowly turned her face his way. Their eyes locked, his cocoa irises merging with the pupils, eyes so dark and turbulent with

unexpected questions. And hers too, seeking answers and maybe reassurance as well.

Until the flare of connecting heat that she remembered from their first ever shared glance, all that time ago, hit her like a blast from a furnace. The flush of warmth low in her belly jumped into life and warned that despite her attempts at blocking out the past she 'knew' this man. In the biblical sense. Knew him too many passionate, mind-blowing times in that brief window of craziness.

A hot cascade of visceral memories flashed over her skin the way it had when he'd explored her with his hands. So long ago.

Heat scorched suddenly sensitive skin and molten memories surged with a thrust of explicit detail in her mind until she tore her eyes away, her breathing fast and her mouth dry. Like falling into a hot spring. Good grief.

How was she going to stay sane for the next ninety minutes, having him there, behind her, the whole way around the tour?

She glanced at Dianne but her boss was taking money at the till. Dianne couldn't help. Shouldn't help. It was Faith's problem.

No. She'd do it. And when this cave trip was over she'd find out what this was all about because she'd done nothing wrong.

As usual, it only took a couple of brief wardrobe adjustments until the adventurers were ready—shame it had felt like hours—and she was glad Raimondo hadn't chosen this moment of waiting to approach. She told herself she was relieved. Very relieved.

Because she would do this on her terms.

Finally, the party reassembled and she directed everyone to the wall hung with helmets and headlamps, where she picked up a large and small helmet from the wall and two headlamps on elastic headbands. 'Grab a light and find a helmet your size—they're grouped small, medium and large—and I'll check your straps and talk about using your lights before we leave here.'

Then she lifted her head and walked steadily over to Raimondo. Practising the words in her head. *This is unexpected. How unexpected. What a surprise.*

'Raimondo.' She handed him the helmet.

'Faith.' Just his smooth utterance of her name with his delicious Italian accent made the gooseflesh lift on her arms—unfortunately her hands were too full to rub the irritation.

'This is unexpected.' That had sounded too breathless and she reined in her control. 'As you can see—' she gestured with the helmet at the group just out of earshot '—it's my responsibility to return all these people safely to the surface.' That came out much more firmly. 'I can't have distractions so we can talk later, if that's why you are here.'

She waited.

'Certainly.'

She nodded. Get away now. 'I hope you enjoy the tour.'

He inclined his dark head. 'I enjoyed it last time.' The 'with you' remained unsaid. She spun away from him and began to check every other person's chin strap except his—she couldn't quite come at that—until everyone was helmeted, including herself.

After the usual jokes and selfie photos, and some fast Snapchat posting by the teens, they left the tourist shop to cross the dry grass in an enthusiastic crocodile of intrepid cavers.

She chewed her lip, a habit she'd tried to break when she was nervous, though it certainly wasn't the cave Faith was worried about. It was Raimondo and her own lack of concentration caused by the tall brooding man at the rear of the line.

She needed to remain focused on the safety of sometimes unwittingly careless people, and of course the safety of the delicate structures and ecosystem of the caverns, and she prided herself on her safety record. Over two hundred successful tours. Which was why she wanted to stay attentive while doing her job.

One tour nearly every week for the last six years. Except for the months of her pregnancy. She glanced back and wished she could have asked Raimondo *not* to join the tour but it was too late for that now.

They gathered at the entrance to the cave. She plastered her game face on. 'You might enjoy knowing a little of the history as you crawl through so you can imagine the past. We'll stop here just for a minute so I can set the scene for you. And don't forget to ask any questions as we go.'

Raimondo smiled grimly and her gut clenched. She had to concentrate.

'Binimirr Caves. Binimirr is an Aboriginal word, in one particular Indigenous dialect, for long hole, and those clans knew of this cave for perhaps thousands of years.' She smiled blindly at the assembled group and launched into her spiel. 'As far as European settlers' history goes, a lone horseman first discovered this limestone ridge and then the caves in 1899. He thought them so spectacular that he told others and they came to see them, despite the lack of roads to Lighthouse Bay at the time. They became very popular.'

There were some nods.

'These intrepid people climbed down with ropes and candles and discovered a cathedral of stalactites and stalagmites and even though it was before roads came here they still felt they could market the caverns for tourism.' She pointed back towards the bus. 'That's what it's like now so you can imagine how rough it was more than a hundred years ago.'

One of the teenage boys murmured a 'Wow' and Faith smiled at him.

'Thirty years after the caves were discovered, these early day entrepreneurs built a stately manor with huge picture windows overlooking the sea, to use as accommodation and enticement for visitors. You can see the ornate gates and driveway to the left when you first enter the car park. Maybe that was why it was honeymooners of the early nineteen-hundreds who were attracted by the mysterious caves, though others still came to celebrate the majestic setting. Later, that lovely old building closed to the public and became a private residence. We have a few old photos of what it used to be like in the kiosk if you are interested.'

She had a sudden forlorn thought of how she would have liked a honeymoon in that old mansion and, despite herself, her glance slid to Raimondo.

If it hadn't been for him making the standard so high she might have been married by now!

Faith shook her thoughts away and looked at the eager faces. Best only to look at them. 'Getting inside the cavern and caves is much easier today than it was then.' She gestured to the railed path. 'For them, after days of jolting rides they finally arrived and lowered each other down on ropes tied to the pepper trees, dressed in suits and hats, women in hoops and skirts.'

She waited for the oohs and ahhs to subside as the group imagined the potential wardrobe malfunctions. 'It took those plucky cavers ten hours of clambering, and no doubt countless torn flounces, to crawl through the caves that now take you an hour to circumnavigate when you use the stairs and boardwalks of twentieth century safety.'

She smiled again and it was getting easier to ignore the man at the back. This was her spiel, her forte, sharing this passion. 'In those days there were no pretty electric lights to backdrop the most magnificent of these natural wonders so far below the surface. Just lamps and candles.' She straightened her helmet. 'Okay. We'll enjoy the views you get today when we return to the gentle paths. But first we'll do some rough terrain ourselves and go deeper than the average tourist gets to see.

'Ready?' At their nods she moved forward to the entrance. 'I'll go first and point to where we're exiting the boardwalk. We slip under the rail to seek out the more remote and unusual areas of the cave. When we return you can take your time once you're back on the boardwalk and really savour the lighted areas of the larger caves.'

She looked around for the most nervous faces. 'Anyone who's feeling a little unsure—you should come up here next to me, with the most confident of you at the back.' The quiet man moved diffidently forward and Faith smiled at him. 'It's worth the effort,' she reassured him.

She noted Raimondo had stayed back and she felt the muscles in her shoulders relax a notch. Okay then. He wouldn't be breathing down her neck. Just watching her the whole time. Not great but better.

She went on. 'When you're traversing the cave please remember to use three points of contact to give you balance. Safety is the most important part of stepping off the boardwalk. As you know, we're heading for the dry riverbed which is more than forty metres below the surface and there's no lights down there.'

A few murmurs greeted that. 'If your heart does start to pound—' she slowed so everyone could hear '—if you can feel yourself becoming anxious, take a couple of deep breaths and remember…' They were all listening. She grinned. 'This is fun and there are more of these tours every week and we haven't lost one person yet.'

A ripple of relieved laughter eased the tension. 'Let's go.' Faith ducked her head and stepped down onto the sloping boardwalk. The air temperature cooled as she moved ahead, not too fast, because she could still remember the first time she'd entered the cavern and her open-mouthed awe of the ceilings and floors, but fast enough to encourage people not to stop until she made the point where they left the wooden planks.

A few minutes later she counted eight adults. 'Right then.' She crouched down, slid under the rail and put her weight on the uneven rocks off the main path, the stones like familiar friends under her feet. Then she slid sideways through a crevice, down an incline, and stopped to point out a particularly wobbly rock and let everyone catch up. 'Try to plant your weight on the big rocks—not into the holes.' She heard the crack of a helmet behind her as someone bumped their forehead. Bless the helmets.

'Now sit down on your bottom to slide off this small drop into the darkness below.' A stifled gasp from right behind her suggested someone had sat down too quickly and hit the wet spot on the cavern floor.

She raised her voice a little. 'It might be time to turn that headlamp on. Shine it on your feet, not into the eyes of the person in front, or into their faces behind you when you turn your head.'

This was all the fun stuff but she knew that most of the tourists behind her would be stamping down the claustrophobia of being in a small tunnel space underground with someone in front and someone following them.

It was lucky Raimondo was at the back because the others might forget how much space he took up. Not something Faith could forget, though for a different reason.

She paused at a fork in the path and waited for everyone to catch up, then pointed at a magnificent curtain of rock.

'That veil of rock is where hundreds of years of dripping water have formed a bacon-rind-shaped rim of curved ice that divides the ceiling.' She remembered enthusing about that to Raimondo all those years ago.

She shook the thought off. The beauty truly did make her astonished every time. Lifting her chin, she pulled her imaginary cloak of confidence tightly around her again. 'Ahead are more joined stalactites to reach towards stalagmites and if you look over here there's a magnificent column that stretches from floor to ceiling. What a gift of nature—that took thousands of years.'

The reverence was back in her own voice because, despite the man at the end of the line of tourists, every time she came down here she shook her head in wonder. Which was why she still marvelled that Dianne actually paid her to savour this subterranean cathedral she loved so much.

They'd come to one of the tricky spots. 'This opening's narrow—be careful not to scrape yourself here.' This was the point she had wondered if Raimondo would have difficulty with sliding through.

He seemed even bigger than when she'd met him before. Hard to imagine but true. More wedge-shaped. Toughened and toned. Muscled and honed. Hopefully not so broad that he'd jam in the crevice like a cork in a bottle—but she had a contingency plan for the others if he did. Not so much for him. She stifled an evil grin. Tsk, Faith, she admonished herself.

Still, there was another, less accessible exit for emergencies, and nobody had ever really been stuck.

Yet.

She waited.

Tried not to hold her breath.

Her heart rate picked up as she heard the subtle crunch of rock fragments in a long agonising squeeze, then he pushed through into the small cavern they were all standing in with a slight rush. Close fit.

Her breath puffed out.

He was fine. Bet that made the sweat stand out on his manly brow though. She smiled.

Then frowned at herself.

Another tsk. Not nice, Faith.

This was unlike her and a measure of how much that grim visage of his had affected her equilibrium.

Stop thinking about him.

'We'll edge down this rock face now. The path narrows so please don't touch that glistening rock there,' She shone her headlamp at the shimmering silver wall. 'It has beautiful fragile crystals so you can take photos and admire it, but it will become disfigured if you accidentally touch it.' She watched them and saw with satisfaction how they all leaned the other way to protect the wall.

'Thank you,' she murmured. 'Almost there.' There were a few Hail Marys behind her and she stifled a laugh. The shy quiet man had turned out to be a Catholic comedian. You had to love him.

Finally, after another ten minutes of winding and uneven descent, she stepped into an opening with a sloping floor. It spread out into a wide cavern and she heard the sighs of relief to be able to spread out a little. The distance narrowed between roof and floor and she resisted the urge to duck her head. Enough of that soon enough.

'If you shine your lights down towards your shoes you'll see you're standing on red sandy soil.'

All lights tilted downwards and there were some comments of, 'All the way down here. Wow.'

'So, we're here. You're standing on the bed of a river from thousands of years ago, stretching away in two directions.'

She let that statement sit in the silence as the others thought about that and shone their headlamps around. 'As you can see with your lights…' and that was all they could see with, as no other light could penetrate this far into the cave '…there's a line of white rocks marking off a section of the cave. Also, in front of us, a circle of the same stones to protect an area of new stalactite formation.'

She crouched down and even now she could feel the excitement as her heart rate sped up with the wonder of all this subterranean world so far below the surface. 'See this—' She pointed out the new holes burrowing into the dirt in the centre of the circle.

'Every drop is making the hole larger and eventually it will form a pencil of creation.'

She breathed out and those standing next to her murmured their own awe. This was why she loved these tours. When she felt the connection from others at the opportunity to see something so few people had.

'If you look across from us—' she angled her head and the light shone on the roof '—hanging from the low roof like eyelashes, those are thin tendrils of tree roots that are searching for the water that left eons ago, but the moisture remains and even though the roots don't touch any water the filaments absorb moisture from the air.'

Someone said, 'Amazing.' She smiled in their direction.

'There's no natural light—the creatures who live here are small, without eyes, their bodies are see-through, almost like albino slaters.' She crouched down and drew an example the size of a cat in the red dirt with her finger.

Her comedian said in the darkness, 'That looks too big for comfort,' and laughed nervously. Several other voices murmured.

Faith grinned. 'Not drawn to scale.' She pointed out a tiny white beetle-like creature on a tree root. 'But if you see one of them in front of you when you're crawling, please scoop up a handful of dirt and shift him aside.'

The young woman next to Faith who'd changed into jeans said in a small voice, 'You say we are crawling?'

'Yep, we're sliding under that overhang on our stomachs, using our elbows, for about thirty metres, but it opens into a small cavern after that.'

'Perhaps,' she said in her lilting accent, 'I can stay here and mind the bags?'

Faith looked at her and noted her pinched nostrils and darting eyes. 'Perfectly fine. We'll only be about ten minutes' crawl away, though you mightn't hear us because the riverbed bends a little. Then it opens into another cavern where we can sit up.

We'll be gone for about thirty minutes by the time we spend ten minutes there as well as crawling there and back. Will you be fine with that?'

She laughed nervously. 'I find it very peaceful here.'

'I'll stay with her,' one of the teenage boys offered with pretended resignation. It was so obviously what he wanted to do that everyone laughed.

Faith nodded. 'The rest of us can drop all our extra stuff, like cameras and jumpers, here. Too hard to crawl on your belly dragging a drink bottle or camera.'

There was a small wave of tense laughter as people dropped surplus bits and crouched down. The black semi-circular opening above the red sandy floor looked about three feet high and maybe ten feet wide, based with the red sand of the ancient river. A little too much like a mouth that would eat them, Faith had thought the first time, and she guessed a few of the others now thought the same.

'I'll go belly down into the damp dirt first so you know I'm ahead, but I need a volunteer to go last. Someone needs to make sure we all keep going.'

'I will go last.' Raimondo spoke quietly, his thick accent rolling calmly around the tiny space. When the others expelled breaths of relief he said, 'I have been on this tour before and have no concerns.'

Faith knew this last stretch tested the first timers' resolve as they slithered forward in the dark, seeing the backside and feet of the person in front, the circle of light from the person behind washing over them, the roof closing in over their helmeted head. She'd had the occasional talk down of a panicked group member at this part but in the end they all agreed the challenge was worth it.

Faith knelt down until she was lying on the damp sand and glanced at Raimondo, looming above her. He nodded calmly and with a last flashing grin at the rest of the group she propelled herself forward along the riverbed, the circle of her headlamp piercing the darkness ahead with its warm glow.

She heard them behind her and the flicker of the others' lights occasionally shone past until she'd crawled all the way to the cavern.

She sat up and waited, watching the circles of light approach one by one as each crawled out of the hole and into the circle of the cavern.

'You can sit up now. There's a good foot over your head.'

'Gee, thanks,' the first arrival, the other of the solid woman's sons, muttered mock complainingly, and she grinned in his direction.

'Just shimmy around so the next person can sit up and move next to you until we have a circle.' It didn't take long for all of them to arrive and she wasn't sure how Raimondo ended up sitting next to her, but she doubted it was by accident.

Faith cleared her throat. She couldn't change the next bit and he probably knew it. 'We're going to turn out all our lights and just sit here, in the belly of Mother Earth, in the dark, and soak in the wonder of what we are experiencing.'

The same smart alec said, 'Why not?' But everyone laughed. Except Raimondo.

There was a murmur of further surprise and then slowly, as they all began to feel the magic of the space, she could feel the agreement.

She pushed on. 'And we'll sit in silence for a minute or two just to soak it in—where we are, how long this cavern has been here, and how amazing you all are to do this and still be having fun.'

A few murmurs of pride.

'After the silence I'll share an Aboriginal legend I was told about a good spirit from the ocean and a bad spirit from the cave, and how these caves were formed.'

Like good children, one by one they turned out the lights until the darkness fell like a blindfold over them.

Faith closed her eyes. She always found this moment, this silence, incredibly peaceful. The air she breathed felt moist on her nose and throat as she inhaled and she dug her fingers into the damp earth and collected two handfuls of the sleeping riverbed and held them with her eyes shut tight—not that it made any difference, open or shut, in the total dark.

She always felt blessed to have been given this moment in time to embrace the idea of being a part of this river under the earth. Breathing in and out quietly as the silence stretched for several minutes. Nobody fidgeted or spoke until she judged enough time had passed. Then she began to tell the story of the battle of the ancients.

CHAPTER TWO

RAIMONDO BRUNO SALVANELLI closed his eyes as Faith's lilting voice rose from the darkness beside him. He allowed her words to flow over and through him because he'd heard the cave story before, privately, and he wanted to find the peace she'd once told him she found here—for himself.

So, instead of listening to the story, he savoured the cadence of her voice and the reality that she had still been exactly where he'd left her so long ago. Again, he inhaled the oh, so subtle scent of her herbal shampoo and welcomed the warmth in the air from her body so close to his.

The sudden rush of possessiveness he'd felt when he'd first seen her from the tourist shop door had shocked him. An emotion he had no right to, a stranger very briefly in her life almost six years ago, a stranger still, and one who had told her he would never return after he had broken her heart.

That first time had been Sydney Airport where he'd caught her eye, she'd smiled, and he'd instantly invited her to join him when he'd seen her flight had been postponed along with his.

Then, hours later, because still he wasn't ready to lose his new companion, they'd shared dinner in an airport bar, jostled by other stranded passengers yet alone in their own world of discovery, and she had captivated him. He'd watched her mobile face as she'd described her beautiful Lighthouse Bay. Her work as a midwife, her hobby of cave tours and her love of life.

Their flights had been rescheduled again and they'd spent the night stranded, and then, imprudently, tangled together making love in an airport hotel, lost to the wild weather outside that had grounded their aircraft.

The crazy urgency had grown until he'd done something so out of character, so reckless and impulsive, even years later he was still surprised. He'd changed his flight to match her re-booked one, delayed his return to Italy for two days, followed her home to the house on the cliff for the one night and two days he hadn't scheduled and found himself lost in unsophisticated and trusting arms.

This was a world of tenderness he hadn't known since he'd been a child and his parents had been alive.

When she'd taken him the next morning for a personal cave tour before he'd left he'd been captivated again by her passion for the natural wonders she'd shared. Had silently begun to plan to return and see where this craziness between them might lead.

Then the return to sanity from the craziness that had come upon him with Faith. He could have vanished into it for ever if not for that call from his brother—his grandfather lay dying, the man who had raised them since he was seven. The news had been a deluge of cold water that had dashed his dreams and dragged him home to filial duty and deathbed requests. His brother had warned him what lay in store so he had said goodbye to Faith with finality.

Never to return because they were from different worlds. Because of the commitment he'd made to his dying grandfather—one he would never have broken until it had self-destructed—his fault, his ex-wife's fault and also partly this woman's fault because his heart had not been available. His new wife had seen that and hardened her own heart even more. Then his twin brother's tragedy and the need for Raimondo to shoulder the leader's role until Dominico could recover.

At the time, returning to Australia had seemed impossible. His brother had agreed that the woman he'd had so brief a liaison with would have married by now, then the years had slipped by so fast after his marriage had dissolved—his new direction into a general practice for the needy, and the occasional international aid work, placating his feelings of failure and he didn't have the time to fly across the world on a whim.

There had never seemed a future, with Faith settled here and him a son of Italy for ever. Had he been wrong?

He would never have come back except for the news he'd heard.

News he hadn't believed.

News he hadn't been able to risk not investigating.

It had been the mention of a place called

Lighthouse Bay in Australia, in a discussion of a wedding one of his colleagues had attended before she'd returned to Florence.

Raimondo had been drawn like a moth to the flame of that conversation.

'So, you have seen Lighthouse Bay?' he'd asked, unable to stop himself.

'Yes, I have been to two weddings there, now. This wedding in the church and one on the beach. Both very beautiful.'

His colleague had appeared mildly curious that he too had seen the place. Again unable to help himself, he had asked about Faith and the answer had stunned him.

'Yes, I met many people. And yes!' There had been an amused glance. 'In fact, I remember Faith, the bridesmaid, and her little girl—so cute.'

He had not known she had a daughter. 'So, she's married then?'

'No, Mr Puritan. She has a daughter without a husband. The child looked about four or five.'

So he'd come.

And on his first sight of Faith, the woman he'd never forgotten but whose charisma had endured as if she were a distant enchanted dream, he'd felt the swell of an emotion he shouldn't have. Here he was, sitting on the sandy bed of an ancient river, forty-five metres below the earth's surface, listening to her so-charming voice as it caressed his ears and wishing he had never left.

That voice was still as restful and as calming. She was as beautiful as he remembered, with her slim but curved body poured into that ridiculous T-shirt and so tight jeans. It proved difficult to resist the urge to slide his fingers through the damp earth and find her hand to take in his, as he had when she'd brought him on a private tour of this place.

His empty hand could even remember the warmth and softness of her small fingers interlaced with his from all that time ago. How could that be? He didn't know. What he did know was that he had not planned well.

A week would not be long enough.

He knew that now from his first sight of her, the way his whole being had come alive from what felt like a deep sleep. And that was without the added possibility that they shared a child.

Faith. He'd lost her and her conviction in the goodness of others and perhaps he would find both again in this place of dark caves and far oceans. He'd forgotten so much about her and he wanted to learn it all over again.

Which would require some negotiation with the life he'd left behind. And his need to encourage his twin brother away from his obsessive focus on the business after losing his family. Raimondo's busy life suddenly seemed far less important than it should, compared to what was happening at Lighthouse Bay.

But that was for later.

He realised the story had finished, the cave silent for those few seconds after a well-told tale, and then soft questions broke out.

Faith answered them quietly then concluded, 'Okay then. Lights on. Those nearest the entrance can start to crawl back and congregate in the next cavern. I'm sure those waiting will be glad to see us. When we make our way back to the main paths and under the rail again, I'll do one more head count then you're free to wander. Just drop your helmets and headlamps back at the shop when you're finished.'

'What if we get lost?' The comedian.

'You'll be on the main path. And they'll switch the spotlights on and off in the cave when it's shutting, so you'll know when we are about to close. In about four hours.' There was a smile in her voice, one he remembered too clearly, and the group laughed.

'I'm used to the dark now,' someone said and the person next to them snorted.

He waited. He knew she would be the last to leave this cavern deep in the earth in case someone became lost or panicked. So he waited with her. As he should have waited before.

Six years! She'd been so young, beautiful, excited and as attracted to him as he'd been to her—the two of them like two silly moths mesmerised by the moment—grounded in an airport cocoon of wild weather and overwhelming fascination increased by the improbability of any future. Once he'd finished his business in Sydney he'd be flying home to Italy, her back to her seaside town and her beloved midwifery. She'd been barely twenty and he eight years senior and should have known better.

But they'd talked until their mouths were dry. Been amazed by the rapport that had sprung between them as if reunited friends from childhood. How could that be? From opposite sides of the world?

From a past life, Faith had said, and he'd hugged her to him for the endearing ridiculousness of that statement.

Though, once she'd laid her head against his chest, it was then that everything had spun out of control. For two full days until his brother had grounded him with familial duty, then he knew their love castles were built on dreams he couldn't follow. Could never follow. A truth he'd left her with. But was that all he'd left her with?

CHAPTER THREE

FAITH WATCHED THE headlamp lights disappear one by one. Damn, she'd missed her chance to send him first.

She tried telepathy.

Go!

She urged the man beside her to move off with the others but he obviously wasn't picking up the vibe. She couldn't go until he had, it was her way, and she broke the silence between them as the last lamp disappeared under the curtain of rock.

'I need you to go now, please.'

He didn't say anything, just moved forward and crawled away from her.

Faith took a moment to breathe deeply and centre herself, and here in the arms of the earth on the soft sand of millennia was a good place to do it.

Okay. She'd get them all back to the safety

of the walking path and then they could talk. She didn't have to pick up Chloe until two p.m., just before work, when preschool finished. So she had a couple of hours to discover why Raimondo had returned to rattle her composure and her world.

She wondered what her aunt would say when she told her Chloe's father had arrived, far too many years too late.

Twenty minutes later she left the group at the boardwalk and her job was done.

Except one of the participants didn't stay behind and she could feel the heat from Raimondo's body as he walked beside her to the exit of the cave. His arm swung beside her arm and she tucked her fingers in close to her body so she didn't accidentally knock his hand.

Out in the bright sunshine Faith stopped on the path and the man beside her stopped too. She lifted her head and met his gaze steadily. 'So why are you here?' She'd done nothing wrong.

His eyes were that deep espresso brown of unfiltered coffee, dark and difficult to see to the bottom of the cup or, more to the point, to the bottom of his heart.

'I have come because I heard you had a child.' His cadence was old-fashioned, she remembered that, formally stiff, but it was a way of speaking she'd found incredibly sexy when she'd been young and silly, in its translated whimsy of sentence structure.

Then his words settled over her like the damp leaves had settled over the forest floor. Thick and stealing the light. He had heard?

She blinked. Pushed back his heaviness. 'I wrote you that. At the beginning and at the end of my pregnancy. Five years ago.'

'No. I did not see this.' He shook his head emphatically, but his face stilled and suddenly expression fled to leave an inscrutable mask of blank shock. 'Madonna.' A quiet explosive hiss.

'Chloe, not Madonna,' she offered with just a little tartness in her voice. She frowned at him. Trying to understand. 'I wrote twice.'

Again he said, 'No.'

He shook his head but he must have seen the truth in her eyes because his face softened slightly as he looked at her. The silence stretched between them until he said softly, 'Then it is as I suspected? You had a child that is mine?'

Unfortunate words if he wanted her to continue this conversation. 'No.' She watched him blink. Good.

He'd relinquished that role by his disinterest. 'You fathered a child who is mine.' She amazed herself with the steadiness and calmness of the answer while her heart bounced in agitation in her chest. 'Her name is Chloe and she is almost five. Chloe Fetherstone.' She needed time to think and her feet moved her forward. He reached out and caught her hand, not tight but with an implacable hold she couldn't shake off without an undignified tug.

She stopped and glanced pointedly at his big fingers on her wrist. 'Let go. I need a minute.' She wasn't the timid junior midwife who'd fallen for him years ago. She was a single mother, a senior midwife, a responsible niece to a woman she admired and who had been the rock this man should have been.

She held his gaze with her eyebrows raised.

His fingers released her.

Faith began to walk again and he fell into step beside her.

He hadn't known?

Had she addressed the envelope correctly?

She'd addressed it so many times until at last she hadn't torn up the letter. He'd told her his home town and she had based her identity search assuming he hadn't lied about that or his true name.

'Where did you send these letters?' His mind must be running along the same lines as hers.

'I looked you up. In the town you'd mentioned. Sent it to your house.' She recited the address. Funny how she could still remember it. She glanced at him. 'Two letters eight months apart. Don't get the wrong idea. I knew where I stood. I wasn't asking for anything. Just giving you information I felt you should have.'

His face had gone back to inscrutable. 'Did you not think it strange when no answer returned?'

'Of course. Though "strange" was not the word I would have chosen. Thoughtless. Uncaring. Bitterly disappointing.' She shrugged.

It was a long time ago now and she was over it. Over him. 'You said you would never return. I expected little. I did my part and it was not my fault if you defaulted on yours.'

'I did not…' His voice had grown harsher, risen just a little. 'Default.' Then the last word more quietly. He looked at her. 'My apologies. This is…difficult.'

She laughed with little amusement. So was meeting a transient lover from years ago when she'd been young and silly enough to fall pregnant. 'Take your time.'

Faith looked ahead to the tourist shop they'd almost reached. 'Give me your helmet and headlamp. I'll get my things and we can go for a coffee somewhere.'

She surprised herself with the stability in her voice when inside she was panicking and fretting. She wished her heart would settle into a cold calm. What did this mean for the world she had created for Chloe and herself? She hated not being in control—even if it didn't show.

No. He would not cast her into turmoil again. She had this. She had to have it. She was comfortable in her shoes as the one who had done the right thing and as a single mother who loved her child more than life itself. He was the one who had had the shock and would have to change the way he thought.

By the time she returned from the shop the tracks he'd made with his pacing showed dirt underneath the mounds of blue metal road gravel. Worn away with his exasperation. She almost smiled at that but if he hadn't known about Chloe at all then she could feel sympathy for his shock. She could still remember that cold horror from the unforgettable day her pregnancy test had shown a positive reading.

Yes, she had sympathy, but no, she wasn't relaxing. She didn't have the luxury of softness or at least she didn't have the headspace for it just yet. Would Isabel think her mad or prudent to let him into their lives? Then again, her aunt was a sensible woman with few prejudices.

'Which is your car?' Hers was way across the car park under a tree and they'd have to drive to Lighthouse Bay for coffee. She didn't want him following her straight to Chloe. They'd go somewhere first. Talk. She wasn't taking him home. Yet.

He indicated the black Mustang Shelby not far from her vehicle, well splattered with dirt and mud from the road into the caves, and even from a distance it seemed to glower at the assortment of vehicles in the cleared space. Like Raimondo had glowered when he'd first arrived. She wasn't taking attitude from either of them, gave the car a disdainful look then caught herself.

Silly, she chided. It was just a rental car and she was getting fanciful, but the model was unusual for these parts. Still, to him she raised her brows. Why was she not surprised he'd hire the most expensive and flamboyant one possible?

Years ago, when she'd searched on the web for him, she'd seen the terrifying extent of his family's influence and power, their pharmaceutical company, backed by a photo of Raimondo and his brother and an elderly, strong-jawed, massive-shouldered man who had to be his late grandfather—long Roman noses making it clear they were all related—and was almost glad she didn't have to meet that old man, that family, and parade her naïveté.

Though she'd decided when Chloe was older she could make the decision for herself as to whether she would contact her father or not and Faith would support her daughter's decision.

Well, that was moot now. He was here to talk about Chloe. 'That car looks like you.'

'How so?' His brow quirked.

'Expensive. Black. Muscly.' She had to smile. 'Low to the ground doesn't fit though.'

He was looking at her as if he couldn't quite work her out. She guessed she had changed from the agreeable, star-struck twit she'd been when she'd met him all those years ago into a seemingly confident woman. No. Not seemingly. She was confident. She wondered if he was having a problem understanding why she had hadn't fallen into hysterics when he'd appeared.

Time to show that maturity she had spent years acquiring. 'We can have coffee at the little café down on the beach at Lighthouse Bay.'

If he'd found her here he could find the town beach. 'I'll meet you there.'

'I will follow you.' He touched her hand and she looked back at him. 'When will I meet our daughter?'

She let the 'our' go. At least he'd shifted from 'my'. 'Soon. After we talk I'll let you know.'

The hard stare that followed her response made her pulse jump a little. She hadn't seen this side of him and she realised they'd both grown up. She reminded herself how he might be feeling and tempered her response. 'It will happen.' *As long as you're good*, but she didn't say that out loud. Might not be polite.

'Faith!' Dianne's voice called out and Faith spun to answer the urgency she could hear in her boss's call.

She jogged back to the shop and could hear Raimondo behind her, which was a good thing when she saw the lovely older gentleman from the cave tour, his iridescent shoes shining up at them as he lay face up on the floor of the shop with his wrinkled face quickly turning blue. Dianne knelt beside the man, shaking him. She had the box with the bag and resuscitation mask beside her but hadn't had a chance to open it. She was fumbling with the catch.

Her eyes were huge. 'He staggered in and then just sagged to the floor. I rolled him over but he's gone blue.'

'Dianne, you ring the ambulance then come back. We'll start here.' Faith knelt down to tilt the man's head and check his airway. She placed her cheek near his nose and mouth but couldn't feel any movement. 'He's not breathing.'

Raimondo nodded and shifted forward to lean over the man and begin efficient cardiac massage. Thank goodness she and Dianne weren't alone to manage until the ambulance came. As quickly as she could, Faith assembled the bag and mask Dianne had left and positioned them over the elderly man's face. She squeezed a breath into his lungs after every thirty compressions that Raimondo made.

After four cycles and no visible improvement they swapped places as Dianne came back. She was puffing from the run. 'Ambulance is on the way.'

'Do you have a defibrillator? An AED?' Raimondo's question made Faith's head lift. She felt like slapping her forehead. Why hadn't she thought to ask for that before Dianne went to the phone? She knew they had one. For every minute the patient didn't respond their survival rate dropped by ten per cent. The sooner the defibrillator was attached the better.

Dianne stared at Raimondo for a second as her brain caught up. 'Yes. On the wall.' She spun around and disappeared then reappeared almost instantly, holding the yellow box with the small Automated Emergency Defibrillator.

'Well done.' Raimondo shot her a smile. 'Can you take over the bagging from me after the next two breaths and I'll take over the cardiac massage from Faith? Count to thirty compressions and then two breaths. Faith can position the defibrillator while we continue on.'

Faith looked at him. Nice. It was exhausting work even though she'd made sure she had her shoulders straight over her locked hands. She was slowing already and Raimondo could make a much more efficient compression of the chest walls than she could when tiring.

She heard the two breaths go in, Raimondo put down the bag and mask and slid in beside her to take over with very little interruption to the rhythm.

Very slick, she thought gratefully as she moved quickly to the man's shirt and pulled it open. Luckily his chest had scarce hair so the connection would be good without the shaving they didn't have time to do. Peeling off the backing paper, she slapped the adhesive pads onto his chest wall above the right nipple and the left pad below the heart.

Switching on the machine, the automated voice intoned 'Stop CPR, do not touch patient, analysing.'

'Clear the patient.' Raimondo's firm voice reminded them not to touch the man in case a rescuer's pulse was counted accidentally by the sensors. Everyone sat back. Raimondo's eyes met Faith's. This was the man's best chance but they also knew that a shock would only be useful if the rhythm was one that could be corrected by an electric surge.

'VT or VF,' Faith hoped out loud as she crossed her fingers.

Raimondo said to Dianne, 'If it says shock, stay back and don't touch him. After the shock we will begin CPR again for two minutes. Then the machine will reassess so we will stop again. If it says "no shock required" we will recommence cardiac massage.'

'I never thought I'd see this thing used,' Dianne said shakily.

'Shock advised.' Said the machine.

'Stand clear,' Raimondo said again and it felt surreal to Faith that a man she hadn't seen for so long sat beside her. Not only that, he'd joined her in a resuscitation in a tourist shop near Lighthouse Bay. Not how she'd seen today pan out, but at this moment she couldn't be happier he was here.

The machine began the warning noises until the patient's body jerked with the surge of electricity and, with an odd gurgling noise, the man's chest heaved as he dragged in a shuddering breath. His eyelids flickered but didn't open.

Faith looked at Raimondo. 'Thank God,' she said at the same time as Dianne murmured the same.

Raimondo's lips twitched. *'Sì.'* He lifted his head and listened. 'The ambulance is nearly here as well.' They all listened to the faint wail in the distance.

Faith narrowed her eyes as she thought about the road in. 'It's a few minutes away. Will we roll him onto his side?'

'Yes.' They did so, the man mumbling something, causing Faith to bend down near his ear.

'It's okay. You've been unwell but you're looking better now. The ambulance is coming and they'll take you to hospital.'

He struggled to open his eyes and when he saw her he sagged back and relaxed, though his hand crept up to his chest. Whether from cardiac pain or bruising to his ribs from Raimondo, she couldn't tell. 'Faith. You. Thank you.'

'We all helped. Lie quietly. The ambulance will bring oxygen and pain relief.'

'Okay,' on an outward sigh as he closed his eyes. She had no doubt he would have some significant pain.

Five minutes later the ambulance arrived and everything moved quickly after that.

Faith left Raimondo to assist and explain to the paramedics and took Dianne into the shop for a cup of tea as the older lady looked shaky after the excitement.

Faith was feeling a little shaky herself. Cardiac arrest was not something she'd seen in the maternity ward, thank goodness, though, because it was possible, they all did their yearly competencies in resuscitation. It was reassuring she'd remembered what to do.

'So lucky we had the doctor here.' Dianne was still coming down from the good outcome.

'Yes. Very lucky.' She'd known Raimondo had finished medicine, but had thought he worked at the drug company, but he'd been as slick as an ED doctor. She guessed she'd find out. Six years was time for many things to change.

'And that you know him,' Dianne enthused. 'He was so calm. And you were too, dear. I'm very glad you were both here.' That last was said a little tearfully and Faith gave Dianne's hand a squeeze.

'You were brilliant too, Dianne. Barney is very lucky. Getting the equipment. Ringing the ambulance and then taking over perfectly while I put the chest stickers on. You were a marvel.'

'We were a good team.' Dianne nodded and lifted her chin.

Raimondo had made the difference out of all of them though, Chloe thought. Cardiac massage was hard work and without his arms beside her she would have been scrambling to get it all done and keep the perfusion up for Barney to give him that second chance.

Raimondo's big hands and strong arms. His presence. So many facets that had captured her so long ago, and she could appreciate them now. But she wouldn't be swayed into softening. She couldn't.

They heard the ambulance leave and Raimondo appeared at the door. Faith kissed Dianne's cheek. 'You did really well. I'll go now if you're okay.'

'I'm fine.' Dianne took a deep breath and plastered a smile on her face. 'A day with a difference, that's for sure.'

Faith glanced at the man at the door. 'Absolutely.'

'You were excellent,' Raimondo said to Dianne. 'As was Faith.' He gestured to the AED, which was in Faith's hand.

'I'll replace the sticky pads from the hospital stores and bring it back.'

He nodded. 'All things we needed done were done.' He inclined his head. 'Thank you.' Smiled his killer smile at Dianne, who blinked and smiled back, half-besotted.

'Thank you, Doctor.'

Faith rolled her eyes. She was getting over the benefit side of Raimondo being there now and moving to the worry.

'Raimondo and I have to go,' she said and led the way from the shop to head across the car park.

CHAPTER FOUR

RAIMONDO'S GAZE REMAINED on her as Faith walked across the gravel of the car park, her tall, willowy body weaving between the parked vehicles with a natural grace that held his eye and made his heart pound. He'd been a fool not to return. And doubly so because of Chloe. If only he'd known.

But Faith? Faith made his heart pound even more than working on a cardiac arrest. *Dios.* What a day. Faith had been magnificent. Of course. He had known the young woman he had left behind all those years ago had strength and today he had seen the growth of that inner steel for himself.

With the resuscitation, the elderly man had been fortunate, and he wished him well. In fact, he would telephone the regional hospital he would be taken to. The paramedics had said they would bypass Lighthouse

Bay Hospital for the more cardiac-focused regional centre. He knew instinctively Faith would want to know as well. Funny how already he was back to considering what Faith would want and including her in his plans.

But this moment, this second in the deserted car park, he could see her dark hair, halfway down her back now that it was loose from the ponytail she'd worn for the tour. Hair that glistened as it captured the sun in subtle red highlights, cascading in a riot of soft waves. He could almost feel the texture of those thick strands between his fingers and frowned at himself.

This was not why he'd come.

For these feelings to reappear was not reasonable. He'd come here because he'd suspected this woman had purposely excluded him from his daughter's life. And why had that been so incredibly painful that he'd boarded the first plane he could?

Probably because in his heart he could not believe that was like the Faith of his treasured memories. And yes, if letters had been sent, and intercepted, twice, with malice or agenda, then it would be like Maria to have done that. His bitter, conceited, forever dissatisfied ex-wife. It would have amused Maria to have caused that loss.

Yes, he believed it of Maria but not of Faith. The last damaging laugh to Maria. With Faith and her daughter the most injured parties.

Faith turned her head as if she'd caught his thoughts and he saw her brows crease. He waved and forced a smile. He needed to reassure her that he had no plans to do anything she didn't want. She did not trust him. Why should she? He had left her with a child and never answered her letters.

Dios.

As if encouraged by his smile, she waved back and climbed into her car and had him fumbling at the remote to open his own car in his haste to follow before she drove out of his sight.

He mused that this too was like the first moment he'd seen her walk by and felt this same sense of urgency to obey his instinct. What was it about Faith that grabbed him by the throat, shoved him by the shoulder, so he had to follow when he was in her orbit?

He slid into the car and turned on the guttural engine. Yes, he'd been self-indulgent with this hire, and not sensible really when he knew he'd be driving out along this dirt road to the caves, he thought as he shadowed her car down the dusty forest road towards Lighthouse Bay. But it was deeply, primitively satisfying to know she would not be able to speed away if she tried to lose him. He had it bad. But she hadn't tried to run.

Faith was as he'd remembered. With the passing of years she'd grown even more beautiful, more poised and personable, which sat well with her good heart. A heart he hoped he could still believe in because he was afraid he'd been fooling himself that he'd forgotten the woman who had captured his attention so easily.

See what he had done with his recklessness.

She had been left with a child.

He had carelessly altered both their futures and hurt the child he didn't know was his by his irresponsible actions. He shook his head as he drove, shadowing her car, unconsciously ready at any moment to pursue if needed.

Yet, despite his unexpected arrival today, she had not criticised him. Faith had spoken to him with kindness and sense; no rancour or revenge came his way when it should. He knew no other woman who would be so generous and honest. He'd met many who had nowhere near her decency.

Again, here was a growing need to understand what it was about Faith Fetherstone that touched him so much, as well as finding out about the daughter he had yet to meet.

When he'd first suspected about the child he'd done his homework. He'd looked Miss Fetherstone up and seen her address remained the same. Had decided on reintroducing himself at the caves because she couldn't avoid him in a group. Had even booked the tour online after confirming with the owner that the guide—*Faith, who had taken him before*—worked that day. Seemed the best way of making sure she'd be there before he'd booked his flights from Florence.

It had all turned out as he'd planned. And now he was to meet his daughter. Children had been his dream for so long but Maria had turned him from any thought of another arranged marriage.

But a child. Almost five? The thought

suddenly filled him with trepidation that he was not worthy.

What if Chloe was afraid of him? He, a big dark-haired Italian man with no skill for children because only one nephew had bounced on his knee—a nephew gone. Coming from a family with everything except the richest prize. The next generation.

He remembered well when his parents had died how it had felt to face the stern grandfather who was to be his and his brother's future. No softness. Just duty. Sadly, he worried his brother was turning into their grandfather.

Imagine if his own daughter saw his grandfather in him.

He shuddered and his hands clenched on the steering wheel until he forced them to relax. He had faith. And Faith. She would help, but first he needed to convince her he meant no harm. He could appreciate the care she took of her daughter and understand the need to confirm his motives before she gave him access.

The problem was—how much access did he really want and how much would be good for his new family?

CHAPTER FIVE

FAITH DROVE STEADILY, trying not to glance too often in the rear-view mirror as she traversed the winding roads to the turn onto Lighthouse Bay Road. The big black car stayed reasonably back but she was constantly aware of the leashed power of the vehicle.

The charismatic power of the stern-visaged driver.

The relentless momentum of being manoeuvred into this meeting by a man she could see expected his own way.

How had he known she was at the caves? How much planning had he done before he'd arrived and how did she make sure she wasn't on the back foot trying to catch up to him?

All thoughts that continued to swirl fifteen minutes later when Raimondo solicitously ushered her into her seat at the beachside café as if she were a flower of extreme fragility.

A tiny pang pierced her composure. She remembered this feeling. This subtle olde-worlde charm of Raimondo. Being the focus of his dark eyes.

Nobody had pulled her chair out for her since, well, since Raimondo, and it did make her feel more feminine than she had for a long time. But then again, maybe someone else might have been equally caring if she'd been interested in looking for an escort. She'd been too busy being a mum and a midwife and ensuring the protection of her family life to risk a relationship.

Or she hadn't found anyone who made her feel as this man did and it wasn't worth the bother.

The reality of how she reacted to Raimondo made her grip the edges of her seat. He looked calm. Calm like she wanted to be, but she'd been working herself up on the drive, she realised.

His ease, and his ability to even glance around approvingly before he sat, suddenly agitated her. With a rising, and possibly irrational, irritation words spilled out as soon as his backside hit the chair. 'So what does your wife think of you coming all the way to Australia on the chance of paternity?' Shut her mouth. At least she'd said it quietly.

Grimaced at herself. Impatience had made her too blunt. To her relief the oblivious waitress arrived and took their coffee orders and when she'd left it wasn't surprising the silence hung between them.

He studied the table a moment longer before looking across at her and she watched his big fingers smooth the pressed shell and sand placemat in front of him without thought. 'My wife and I annulled our marriage after one year.' His tone remained matter-of-fact though there was an emotion which she couldn't identify lacing the dry words. 'Our legal commitments were met with regard to my grandfather's wishes and it was not required to continue.'

'Annulled?' Legal commitments? But the first part remained her focus. She couldn't help the disbelief in her voice. Her memories did not include a celibate Raimondo. Or a cold-blooded legal brain.

The whirlwind that had been their relationship had exploded into mutual, foolish abandon. Embarrassing in retrospect;

though she could never regret her beautiful Chloe, she did regret her trust in this man. And he hadn't even made the woman he'd left her for happy?

Maybe she, Faith, had had a lucky escape.

'So does annulled mean something different in Italy?' How could they be married for a year and not sleep together?

He shrugged. 'I have little knowledge of your Australian laws. My grandfather in Italy was set on our marriage to combine the two great houses through our offspring. A pact of long standing. Without children the company would move from Florentine control to a Roman cousin. As this was his dying wish, and my brother and his wife had not yet conceived, I met his demands with little choice and speed before he passed—as I explained when I left.'

He'd left like a shot from a gun. 'At the time you said your life was in Italy and you were marrying because of a previous arrangement.' Might have been nice to know that before she'd invited him home.

Her shiny Italian hero had left without looking back. Her turn to wave away the past. 'That's all in the past. Now you're saying you never slept with your wife?' Really? Not the Raimondo she'd known.

'No.' He raised one brow and she decided he did it with a hint of satirical amusement at her expense. She narrowed her eyes. 'The marriage was annulled for infertility not disclosed—not celibacy. My ex-wife is barren. She did not tell me she had been forced by her father to wed or that she had known with certainty of her infertility. As my late grandfather's wish for our marriage relied on children, that made for reasonable grounds for annulment.'

And boy, did that sound horrible and cold. She rubbed her suddenly chilled arms. And this was her daughter's father? So she'd been lucky he'd been called away then. His unemotional recital made her wonder if his wife had been so dispassionate at being deemed unworthy. She shuddered. Like her mother and the small child Faith had been were deemed unworthy when her own father had left.

Her revulsion must have shown on her face because he said, 'Do not judge me for this. Maria never wanted me. She left with more wealth and has found a new husband. I wish her well.'

'Big of you.'

'Especially as she was unfaithful during our marriage.' Then he waved in the air. 'Pah!' He waved again, obviously annoyed with himself. 'This is not your concern. I find myself baring my soul to a woman I barely knew six years ago and again today. Forgive me.'

He was cross with himself all right. If he hadn't looked so sinfully sexy during his sudden almost-tantrum she would have laughed. But his honesty shone through the big hand that pulled regretfully over his face. Maybe she hadn't been as ridiculously blind as she had thought all that time ago. No, don't go there. Things were very different now.

She lifted her chin. 'My fault for asking. But at least I know a little more of you.' Though she didn't really. Except… 'You really didn't get my letters?'

'No. I am sorry.' His brow furrowed. 'Though I can guess who did.'

She supposed so. 'Your wife?'

He shook his head with more regret. Not helpful to Chloe, though. 'Hard to understand Maria could be so cruel, but she felt the lack of children greatly and resented our marriage even more.' He looked at her. 'I'm sorry I wasn't there when you needed me.'

No, you weren't there, she thought, but she could see why he hadn't been. 'My aunt Isabel was there for me. She's still my rock. Though younger than my mum, she stood as my mother's rock as well. We manage very well together.'

'No need for others?' He asked the question with a bitterness she didn't deserve.

'We manage very well. Thank you,' she agreed with composure that was slipping a little. Sadness for her daughter had tightened her throat.

A comedy of errors, five years of her daughter's life, and he was the loser if he'd wanted to be involved. And maybe it hadn't been all his fault. She'd lost as well because even if they'd not ended up together she suspected this man would have been an attentive dad to her little girl as much as he could, considering the physical distance between their two countries.

As in the past, their thoughts seemed to mesh. 'Tell me about your pregnancy. Her birth. Her infancy.' His eyes softened. 'About Chloe. Your daughter.'

Her daughter. Not his. He was trying to

see her side too. But she couldn't soften too much. Couldn't trust that much yet.

Where did she start? 'Chloe was born here at Lighthouse Bay Hospital. A beautiful water birth. It was the most amazing day of my life.' Her eyes misted with the memory. The recollection of those first moments with the weight of her new daughter, pink and wet, heavy between her bare breasts. The scent of her, the downy head and snuffly noises against her skin and the glory that was the wonder of birth.

Her own pride in her achievement. She would never forget that. But that was all too private. Instead she said, 'It will be her birthday soon. She'll be five in two days.'

He leaned forward, his face lighting. 'Two days?'

'Seventeenth of November.'

'May I be there for her birthday?' Nice of him to ask, but she wasn't a fool.

She had no right to bar him, despite her misgivings. She didn't believe he'd cause trouble but to be wrong would be bad. 'That's up to you.' She met his eyes. 'And up to Chloe. And how long you plan on staying might be nice to know as well.' She lifted a hand, palm up, in question.

'A week. I have given myself a week. I fly out next Friday.'

She could do a week. If his family didn't call him back. Ha!

Could protect herself for a week as well.

Protect herself against the chemistry between them that she could still faintly feel, even through the thickest wall she could erect and had become very good at maintaining ever since Chloe's birth.

Then he would be gone and her life would, hopefully could, return to normal. She wasn't moving to Italy and he wasn't moving to Lighthouse Bay so all would sort in the end.

He sat back. Studied her with that intense expression on his face. 'What is she like? This daughter of ours?' Avoiding discussion on what happened after he flew away again, but she guessed nobody knew the answer to that yet.

Knowing the extent of his stay was solid ground, as was the topic of Chloe. She could talk of her daughter until the sun set. 'She's dark-haired and strong…' *Like you*, the thought flashed through her brain, but a wholly feminine version of Raimondo's darkness.

She went on, '… With green eyes and long lashes.'

'Like you.' She lifted her head at the echo of her thoughts and she heard the smile in his voice as he said it.

Maybe. 'She's a minx who gives us pleasure in her company every single day.' She shook her head at the memories that swirled like bright confetti when she thought of her daughter. 'To hear her funny little cackle of a witch's laugh is to know the joy of being a parent.' She stopped. Could have snatched back the thoughtless cliché. 'I'm sorry. Poor word choice in the circumstances.'

He waved that away, still watching her face with an intensity she found discomfiting. 'You love her dearly.'

'More than life itself.' Twice today she'd had that thought and a cold foreboding washed over her. She shivered and his hand came across the table to touch hers.

'I would never do anything to hurt you or Chloe,' he said softly. Sincerely. His eyes held her gaze like his fingers held her wrist and warmth flooded over her. 'Never.'

She nodded. 'I hope I can believe you.' But still the feeling of foreboding didn't go away.

She changed the subject and eased her hand free. 'Where are you staying?'

He gestured to the hill with the same hand. 'In the guest house down from the hospital.'

She knew it well. 'Our locum doctors stay there.'

'Do they?' He smiled at her. 'And how is your little hospital that you loved so much?' As if again sensing her need to regroup.

A safe topic she could also talk about for hours. 'Grown. We birth over a hundred babies a year here now.'

'Then you must have found more doctors to carry on. There were staffing hardships before.'

'A lot has changed since you were here.' And wasn't that an understatement. Her. Their daughter. She thought about the new families in Lighthouse Bay. Her wonderful circle of friends that grew with each new relationship.

'We are a midwife-led unit now, so doctors come only for the general patients and obstetric emergencies.'

He smiled. 'I would be redundant already.'

'You never planned to work here.' Wouldn't

that be a hard thing for her to come to terms with if he was here all the time? Crikey.

He inclined his head. 'As you say. I never planned this. Though I have been doing locum work since my wife and I parted. In poorer suburbs in Italy. A little aid work in Third World countries. My brother has occasionally forgone the pens of the pharmaceutical business and has sometimes joined me in aid work.'

She remembered he had mentioned his work doubts even when they'd met. His new focus helped her to relax a little more when he added, 'The work is much more satisfying and demanding to fill my life. I regret that even your Lighthouse Bay receded into a moment in time.'

Then he could have come back after his divorce, she mused. Come back at least to see if what they'd experienced really had been as special as she'd thought.He'd decided not to, obviously. But things worked out, or didn't, as the case might be, for reasons no one knew, she told herself. Out of sight, out of mind, she supposed a little drearily.

'Tell me what else has changed in this place you love so much over the years.'

She wasn't sure what he was thinking now but she ploughed on, relieved to have a lighter topic to discuss. 'My boss, Ellie, has married, and my friend, Catrina, as well.'

He lifted his head. 'Ah, Catrina.' He smiled and she tilted her head to understand why Trina's name had brought amusement.

He went on, 'It was this Catrina's wedding that brought me here. One of my colleagues at the hospital came to this wedding. She is a friend of Sam's sister and was back visiting—apparently she was at Sam and Ellie's wedding too, and mentioned to me about you and your Chloe.'

Faith stared at him. Trina's wedding? A guest from his town in Italy? 'Mentioned my daughter and me?' There had been some Italian doctors, friends of Sam's sister, but she'd thought them from the city. Surely not. 'Who was your colleague?'

'Francesca Moran. I heard her mention your Lighthouse Bay and I asked after you.' He spread his hands depreciatingly. 'It had been so long since I'd heard of this place so of course the name called to me.' He shrugged and there was a decidedly amused glint in his eyes. 'And, of course, my…' he paused as if searching '…ears prickled?'

'Ears pricked up. Yes.' With a little impatience. 'Why?' She tried to remember if he'd met Trina before. But their intense relationship/liaison had been so short and all-encompassing she didn't think they'd left her cottage except to go to the cave.

As some of those very intimate recollections intruded her face warmed and she looked away. She'd had these memories locked up so long she'd almost forgotten the details. If she let herself relive how it was she might not sleep for a week.

Thankfully, Raimondo seemed to have missed her embarrassment and tutted as if impatient with the subject. 'I asked if she'd seen you and she remembered yes, because your daughter Chloe had been very pretty and had been chasing the tiny flower girl of Trina's husband.'

Faith remembered, though it was more than a year ago. Chloe had been adorable, as had Trina's stepdaughter Piper, and some of her embarrassed confusion seeped away and was replaced with maternal pride. 'She was charged with looking after Piper. And yes, Piper was only two and the flower girl. Chloe can be very responsible for her age.'

He smiled at her obvious pride. 'Of

course she is. She will be composed like her mother.'

She didn't know about that—she was feeling anything but composed at this moment and she needed to get this conversation back on steady ground.

'And because of this you came?'

'Because of this I came.'

Nope. She didn't understand. 'I could have been married with many children.' But she wasn't, mostly because of the impact he'd had on her life, not something she'd dwelt on but she thought of it now. And narrowed her eyes at him.

A shadow crossed his face. 'As you say. Though I was told otherwise. My friend knew you had no husband and Chloe's age made me wonder.'

Obviously, it had made him wonder. 'Wonder enough to cross the world and see?'

'Yes.'

She watched his face. 'And did you investigate further?'

'As you say.' His expression remained unreadable. She decided he was being deliberately vague. 'I owe you many apologies,' he added.

Like that would help, she thought, but she'd decided against stewing in bitterness a long time ago. It changed nothing and she refused to colour her own and Chloe's lives with negative thoughts. That philosophy had stood her in good stead and she wasn't being driven by someone else to change now.

He asked quietly, 'Is there a special man in your life?'

She blinked. Guessed she could understand why he would ask as he'd just exploded into their world. She could say yes. As protection against the tendrils of attraction this man was already curling around her like wisps of smoke. She was fighting it but she had past experience that his illusion of smoke could lead to a sudden flame.

But she wasn't into lying either… 'No.' She lifted her head. 'Not at this time.' Apart from him, there hadn't been a man in her life, really. A few brief ones in uni. Before that, as a child, the father she could barely remember, who had left her mother and her. But she wasn't telling him that. 'Just male friends. And husbands of my friends.'

Her eyes met his and she explained lest he think it was all about him. 'It's better for

Chloe that I don't expose her to the whims of a passing relationship.'

She still didn't know what it had been about Raimondo that had penetrated her barriers years ago—why had she, as a young naïve woman, brought this stranger from another land into her home, to all the places that were dear to her and allowed him access to her heart? To her body?

Because of the magic. And that was the torment of it. Spending time with Raimondo had been like sprinkling fairy dust over her world until she'd felt alive and aware, hyper-sensitive to the beauty all around her. She'd been caught in the bubble of his admiration and returned it to him tenfold. She wouldn't do that this time.

She looked across at the beach in front of her, frowning at it. Even now, the ocean seemed bluer than it had been this morning, the flowers in pots brighter, the sounds of the waves more clear. It was fainter, but she could feel that magic now. Again. Looked back at him as he sat back in his chair and studied her too.

In the past this man had soared into her life like a comet, searing away her reserves, and she knew what had happened the last time with the heat of their collision at the airport. But then he'd rocketed straight out again.

Oh, she was over her feeling of abandonment but she didn't want that for Chloe. No way.

Not really surprising she hadn't rushed into making herself vulnerable to a man again. Not bitter. Just not open to trusting closeness again.

She expanded on her answer, letting him know where her priorities lay. 'I will give Chloe all my time until she starts school before I see if I want to cultivate a man's company on a more permanent basis.'

He raised his brows as if she'd said something vaguely unsettling but he closed his mouth and silence fell between them.

To fill it she said, 'My need for male company has been easily satisfied by social outings with my friends and their husbands or the families of the babies I've welcomed.'

He nodded. 'Then this is good as it is not confusing for Chloe during my visit.'

He was concerned about her daughter's feelings and, against her better judgement, she softened towards him again. A tiny voice whispered plaintively that it was only because of Chloe he was glad there was no another man.

Then she pulled herself up. No. Now she could feel the heat in her cheeks again, damn him. This was how he had managed to get under her guard last time, with solicitude and care and treating her as if she were a princess he needed to guard from the world. Something she'd had no experience of from a man.

And hadn't that changed when his brother had called?

Oh, yes.

She knew where she really stood. Just a phone call and he'd be gone. Not his fault. Oh, no. But family calls…

Her aunt had always said that for the Italian men their family was everything. Well, she had a family, Chloe and Izzy, and she needed to make sure her daughter was safe from the disappointments an unreliable father could bring to her life, so she wasn't falling for his transient solicitude again until he'd proven himself. She would be calm. Careful. Consistent in her barriers.

Who knew what crisis would make him leave next time? She would protect Chloe from the devastation she could suffer when his larger-than-life presence disappeared in a moment. She knew how it felt and Chloe would too in seven days' time. Faith needed to be clear on expectations with Chloe ASAP.

But it was so strange talking like this with a man she'd thought she would never see again.

He'd been watching her silently and she wondered if he could read her thoughts and if they'd crossed her face for him to see. 'What of your friends in your life? Will they be worried that I have come back?'

Did he think it odd she had no man in her life? It could have been tricky if she'd had a boyfriend.

'All my male friends are married to women I care about. Though my aunt has been hinting that when Chloe starts school I should look to building more…adult friendships outside my work.' She looked at him. 'I might look at that then.'

Raimondo glanced around pointedly. 'And no single men have been clamouring at your door? Are they blind not to want to capture you for themselves?' He looked so pleased with her lack of suitors her irritation rose.

She gave him a level stare. 'I've been a fool once. So, of course, I'm reluctant to go there again.'

He winced. 'Of course.'

They'd finished their coffee and she glanced at her watch. It was lunch time. 'I have to go. I need to be at work by two-thirty for the afternoon shift.'

He glanced at his own watch but his face remained difficult to read.

There was a tense pause and finally she said, 'I'm off duty tomorrow.' For Sunday and Monday as well, but she didn't add that. 'If you'd like to come and meet Chloe and my aunt, Isabel, then you could come for breakfast at eight. We could go down to the beach after, as Chloe likes to have a play in the water when she can.'

'Thank you. I would like that. Your aunt cares for Chloe while you work?'

'Yes.' She raised her chin. 'It would have been very difficult without her help.' Again, she noted his grimace of distress, but she'd said it more to show appreciation of her aunt than to make him feel bad. 'Izzy moved in with me just before Chloe was born. She was my mother's youngest sister and only fifteen years older than me and we are our only family. She's put her life on hold for Chloe and me.'

'I imagine there is much closeness between you.'

'There is. Very much. Next year, when Chloe goes to school five days a week, Izzy will be less tied and I'm going to shift to night duty again, which I did in the beginning. There's a young woman from the preschool who has agreed to sleep over with Chloe when I'm at work if Izzy is away. I'll be home to send her off to school and there when she comes back.'

He shook his head. 'I do not like to hear of these hardships inflicted unknowingly on you by my lack of responsibility. I owe you and your aunt a great debt.'

'No. You don't.' No way was he finding a foothold there. 'I love Chloe and there are lots of mothers juggling similar schedules and worse. I get help and wonderful support from my friends as well as Izzy.'

His brow furrowed at being thwarted. A bit too used to getting his own way, she mused, as he said, 'I hope to have some input. But we have time to see.'

She said steadily, 'I've been extremely fortunate and need nothing from you.'

Now his face appeared bland. 'Perhaps this is for another discussion.'

She met his eyes. *Oh, yeah? Let it go, Faith*, she told herself. When she didn't reply he half smiled as if he knew it was her restraint not her change of mind that kept her quiet.

He inclined his head. 'Thank you for your invitation and I will see you at eight tomorrow.'

She did need to get away to think. 'Do you remember where I live?'

He laughed with little amusement. 'Before the cliff. To the left of the crofts. The siren's house above the sea. I remember.'

She laughed. 'I've never been a siren in my life. I'm afraid your memory tricks you.'

One dark brow rose. 'Does it?'

CHAPTER SIX

FAITH DROVE TO the preschool and picked Chloe up way too early. Her daughter didn't see her enter the brightly festooned, noisy room because she sat with her tongue pushed against her teeth as she glued a black felt eye onto a cotton wool ball with fierce concentration.

Her two dark pigtails bounced as she nodded her head to something the little girl beside her said but her attention remained fixed on her task. Chloe was always surrounded by little friends and Faith wondered who she'd inherited her outgoing personality from.

Perhaps Raimondo.

'Chloe, I've come to pick you up.'

'Mummy?' Chloe looked up from her work and her face shone her delight at seeing her mum. She put down the cotton wool ball and jumped up. Threw out her arms. 'My mummy is here. I have to go.' She glanced around the room as if to be sure everyone could see how special the occasion was. Her daughter bounced up and down at the exciting change in routine and happily gathered her new paintings and crafts.

Faith met the amused eyes of the preschool teacher and they both smiled. Chloe ran to the teacher, hugged her, and then back to her mother and caught her hand. 'Let's get my bag.'

Faith savoured the warmth of the little hand in hers, the chatter floating up and the skipping of her daughter's feet as they walked to the car. Her Chloe sunshine.

At least Faith would get home with extra time before work to get her head together. Dashing out to preschool pick-up just before starting shift would have jumbled her thoughts again and she was jumbled enough.

As soon as Faith walked into the little house on the cliff her aunt's dark brows rose and her green eyes widened. Isabel or Aunty Izzy as Chloe called her, didn't miss much. Yup. She knew something had happened.

Izzy took the preschool bag from Faith's slack hand and received her kiss from

Chloe. 'Your sliced pear and milk is in the fridge, darling,' she said, pointing the little girl towards the sink and towel waiting for her small hands without taking her eyes off Faith.

As Chloe happily followed routine, Izzy touched Faith's shoulder and concerned eyes searched her face. 'You okay?'

Was she okay? She'd been solid as a rock while she'd been with Raimondo but at this moment she felt weak at the knees.

'Raimondo Salvanelli turned up at the caves this morning.' The words sounded strange even coming from her own mouth. Spreading her hands helplessly, Izzy didn't appear enlightened.

She'd get it. 'He didn't know about Chloe and someone at Trina's wedding mentioned us and he flew in from Florence.'

Izzy's eyes widened. 'The Italian from the airport?' Then she mouthed silently, 'Chloe's father?'

Faith sank onto the sofa, her eyes drawn to her daughter happily setting her own table, playing house with her milk and fruit on her child-size table setting.

'How could he not know? You wrote. Twice.' Izzy manfully tried to catch up.

Faith turned back to her aunt. 'He said he never received the letters, though the address I sent the letters proved correct. And his marriage has been annulled.' She waved her hand impatiently. 'Long story.' She looked at Chloe again. 'He's coming tomorrow morning at eight.' Lowered her voice. 'To meet Chloe.'

'Who's coming to meet me?' a bright voice piped up. Chloe proved she might be quietly doing her thing but she wasn't oblivious to the tension at the other side of the room.

Faith and Izzy exchanged looks. 'One of mummy's friends from a long time ago is coming to visit tomorrow for breakfast. Of course he'd like to meet you too.'

Chloe's bright eyes studied them both. 'Does your friend have a little girl?'

'Not yet.' Another frazzled look at Izzy from Faith. 'But I think he'd like one.'

Izzy made an inarticulate sound and turned away so Chloe couldn't see her expression. She turned back to Faith, her face composed. 'Well, then. Much excitement.' She glanced at the clock on the wall. 'Why don't you go have a nice freshening shower? Chloe and I will make lunch while you get ready for work.' Her aunt looked at her. 'Unless you don't feel up to going?'

That was more of a joke than a question because Faith would have to be dying to not turn up for work.

'I'll be fine. And yes, thanks, a shower would be good. A strategy for dealing with this, so all will become clear.'

She smiled ruefully at her aunt. 'I might bash my head against the wall a few times, so ignore strange sounds.'

Just before two-thirty that afternoon Faith walked through the glass doors of the Lighthouse Bay Mothers and Babies Wing of the tiny hospital and slipped her bag into the cupboard underneath the desk.

When the world was going crazy thank goodness there was work.

The ward seemed quiet and nobody sat at the desk. She let a small sigh of relief escape her. It would be nice to settle into the shift before the ward focused on an impending birth but she knew what to do regardless when she was here. Unlike in her social life at the moment. She could hear a baby crying so at least they had inpatients. She didn't want it so quiet she needed to work elsewhere in the hospital, which they sometimes did between rushes of babies. She didn't have the head space for that today.

Today there had been too many upheavals in her peaceful private world and the question marks for the future unsettled her in a way she hadn't felt for many years.

Raimondo had the knack of that.

'Hey there, Faith.'

Ellie appeared from one of the side rooms on the ward with a grizzling baby tucked under her arm. The manager of the ward, and sometimes the whole hospital, Ellie preferred when she could work as a hands-on midwife, like today.

'Hi, Ellie.' Her boss looked so happy. 'How's your day been?' Not like hers, that was for sure.

'Excellent. Apart from this baby, who seems to have missed the rules on settling after a feed—but I have the technology—new nappy.'

She looked calm and content carrying the little football baby under her arm, the baby's neck securely supported by her cupped hand. She smiled a warm welcome.

Faith tried to smile back but a sudden unexpected fear that she'd never be like

Ellie, with a man who worshipped her and a proper family, assailed her. A fear she'd never had before, and shouldn't have now, made her realise how much Raimondo had punctured her serene balloon of existence she'd floated in until now.

Her boss was very, very happily married to an obstetrician. Sam consulted at their regional referral centre and not Lighthouse Bay, but he did emergency calls when needed here. Having Sam in the wings was one of the reasons their birth rate had risen so much.

Faith's mouth opened. 'Chloe's dad turned up this morning at the caves.' She slapped a hand over her mouth. She had not meant to blurt that out. What was wrong with her?

Except for a slight pucker of her forehead, Ellie's demeanour didn't change. 'I have supreme confidence in your good sense, Faith. Come into the nursery while I change this poo-bottomed boy. Then I'll give you a handover of our one patient and you can tell me all about "him".'

Faith followed her into the nursery, a space with wide sun-filled windows, a soft chair for breastfeeding mothers and tall benches for dressing and bathing babies. Ellie flipped out a fresh bunny rug and gently eased the little boy down until his head was resting on a folded cloth and began to unwrap him. Faith reached for the cleaning wipes to help and then, noting the disaster uncovered, instead wet a cloth nappy and handed it to Ellie, who laughed.

'Yep. I think we need the big guns to fix this mess.'

She smiled down at the baby as she swiftly righted the world. 'So, this is Jonathon, born this morning at seven-thirty to Maurine McKay.'

Faith felt the smile as it stretched her face. 'Little Maurine?' Maurine barely topped a metre and half tall, though her body was all curves and perfectly proportioned. 'How cool.' Faith shared her midwifery case load with Ellie so she knew Maurine well. 'And was it as easy for her as her last one? She was worried.'

'He flew out,' Ellie said. 'She was here about an hour, not saying much, then she did that thing she did with you last time. You know. The stare. And lay down and had him. The woman is a marvel.'

Faith shook her head in awe. 'Some mums are just designed to have babies. Probably helps that her husband is not much bigger than she is.'

'That too, maybe. Maurine's well, no damage, no extra blood loss, and this young man weighed three thousand grams so a nice size for her.'

Faith calculated quickly. 'About six pound six? Her biggest yet, then. Can't wait to congratulate her.' Faith could feel the tensions of the day falling away from her. This was the world she loved and she felt the calming of her lost equilibrium as it settled over her.

'She's looking forward to seeing you.' Ellie rewrapped the now clean baby. 'So. He's fed twice already, his temperature and respirations are normal and he's going to settle for a good sleep now.' This last was said firmly to the baby, who lay quietly with big dark blue eyes gazing steadily at Ellie.

Ellie picked him up. 'I'll take him back to mum and you pop the kettle on. Then you can tell me about your interesting day.'

By the time Ellie had left the ward and Faith had settled Jonathon again with his boisterous siblings and parents in Maurine's room, she was feeling like herself.

Okay. It had been unexpected—she

snorted at that and the memory of her first greeting to Raimondo—and decided there was nothing she could do so she would take the benefits provided.

Mentally she ticked them off.

At least her daughter would remember a man called Raimondo when she was asked about her father.

Chloe would have some rapport to build on if she went to meet him one day in Italy when she was grown.

Raimondo could write to Chloe and possibly, though she was still thinking about this, contribute to Chloe's senior school or university in later life if he wished—because education was the best gift to give anyone.

She had to admit Raimondo still seemed the lovely man she'd become briefly infatuated with and, yes, she did feel she could trust him with contact with Chloe from the little she'd seen today. But that didn't mean she would.

She wasn't so sure she could trust herself, so she would be vigilant in guarding her good sense and her heart.

They'd do Christmas cards and maybe phone calls on birthdays—surely he could manage that, though she wasn't sure, and in this initial visit he'd be here for Chloe's birthday at least. Faith would put out the albums of Chloe's childhood for him to see.

She sat back. Yes. All ordered in her head nicely.

Chloe would probably enjoy showing Raimondo her photos over and over again. Faith wasn't so sure she was okay with some of the birth ones but, then again, he had seen her naked before.

Oh, my goodness. Quickly she picked up a pen and began to write out the diet list.

The sound of a car arriving in the driveway outside the ward had her out of her seat. Someone in labour?

Then she saw the sleek black Mustang. What the heck…?

Raimondo's big form climbed out and strode to the passenger seat and now Faith could see the shape of another person through the darkly tinted windows. She proved to be a woman and heavily pregnant. Where had Raimondo found a pregnant woman?

Faith grasped the handles of the wheelchair they left tucked handily behind the corner to the birthing rooms and pushed it towards the now opening door. The woman limped in on an obviously tender right leg and held her stomach.

Yep. In labour. Raimondo had brought her to the right place. His words carried. 'Traffic accident.'

What traffic? Faith thought, but she hurried over. The woman leaned on the door as she waited for Faith to park the chair next to her.

'Can you sit down?' Faith held the chair and Raimondo helped her settle into the chair. 'I'm Faith, the midwife on duty.'

'Cynthia Day. My husband is hurt and going in the ambulance. This man said he was a doctor and thought I should come here. Just until the ambulance is ready to leave and can take me too.' She glanced at Raimondo ruefully. 'I've had a few labour pains.'

'I saw the accident and called the ambulance,' Raimondo said. 'Her husband is stable but there may be a delay before they extricate him and are ready to leave. It seemed better to bring Cynthia to be checked before transfer.'

She looked at him. 'Yes. Good thinking. There's at least an hour's road trip in the ambulance so very sensible.' Then to the woman, 'When is your baby due?'

'Four weeks tomorrow.'

Technically premature, Faith thought, but not perilous. 'We'll check you both out and have the ambulance call here to pick you up. I'll pop you through into the assessment room, which is where we have our babies here. Is that okay?'

'Of course.'

Faith turned the chair and began to push it the other way towards the birthing rooms. Raimondo followed and Faith allowed him for the moment. It wasn't as if he was a stranger to hospitals and she'd keep an extra pair of hands until she could get help.

'Have you been here before?' She spoke from behind the woman as her brain sorted priorities.

She didn't recognise the woman and thought she knew all the ladies booked in to give birth at Lighthouse Bay. So medical or obstetric history might not be available.

'No. We're having the baby in Sydney.'

'That's fine. We can get your notes from there.' She'd have them emailed through once Cynthia had signed the release of information form. Or the supervisor could arrange all that because Faith would be busy on her own.

Cynthia sighed. 'We were going home after visiting relatives when my husband took a funny turn at the wheel. I grabbed the steering wheel but it was too late. We ran into a low wall and the front of the car crumpled in, making it difficult to get him out.'

Unlucky. And scary as a risk for possible hidden pregnancy-related trauma. Risk even from the sudden stop. 'Did you hit your stomach?'

'No. The seat belt jerked me when we hit, but that's all.'

Faith nodded to herself. She would have to watch baby for any signs of distress which could be a shearing bleed from the placenta. 'Was the car going fast when you hit?'

'No. I think John must have known something because he hit the brake just before he went unconscious.' She swivelled her head and looked at Raimondo. 'I'm so worried about him. When can you ring and find out how he is?'

'Dr Salvanelli will be able to do that soon.' She knew there was a good reason she'd subconsciously wanted Raimondo to stay. He'd been helpful already.

'Of course,' he said.

Raimondo and Faith stood on each side of Cynthia, supporting her until she was comfortably sitting upright on the bed, the back raised and one pillow supporting her head.

Faith turned to Raimondo as he stepped back. 'Thank you. I'll make a call and a nurse should be here soon. Will you stay by the desk in case I need you before anyone else arrives?'

'Of course.'

'Thank you. It's a good place to find out about Cynthia's husband. The ambulance control number is in red above the desk. They should be able to give you some information if you explain to them or they'll call you back. Tell them we have Cynthia here and expect her to be transferred as well.'

'Sì.'

Faith crossed to the phone in the room and quickly dialled the hospital supervisor. She tucked the phone into her neck to free her hands and twitched the cover off the baby resuscitation trolley, then reached to turn the heater to warm just in case. She'd only checked the equipment half an hour ago, an early in the shift task everyone completed, so she knew everything was ready if they needed it.

'Yes?' the supervisor answered.

'Hi, it's Faith in Maternity. We have an admission, a lady in a car accident. She's stable but contracting and could be in early labour. Can you send over a nurse as my second, please, and phone for Dr Southwell senior? There's an out-of-town doctor here at the moment, so tell the nurse that's who's at the desk when she arrives. Too busy to explain just now.'

She paused. Listened. Said 'Thanks' and put down the phone. 'Right then, Cynthia. Let's have a gentle feel of your tummy and listen to your baby. Raimondo will tell us as soon as he hears any news of your husband.'

Cynthia nodded, her face shining pale against the white pillow, her dark eyes concerned as she held her stomach. 'There's another contraction.'

Faith knitted her forehead. She needed obstetric history soon but the nurse could follow that up when she arrived. Faith crossed to the sink and washed her hands then went back to the bed, drying her fingers on the paper towel. She lowered the bed until Cynthia was lying flat with just the pillow under her head. Palpating a uterus in the upright position wouldn't give the clear picture she needed from an unknown woman.

'Is this your first baby?' They'd have more time if it was, she thought; the contraction had finished as she lifted the pretty blue maternity shirt and gently began to palpate the woman's stomach. Not her first baby, judging by the older silver stretch marks. She laid her fingers each side of the bulge and palpated in Leopold's manoeuvre. 'Nothing painful when I do this?'

'No.'

Good. Less chance of a quiet bleed from the accident then. The height of the uterus was consistent with thirty-six weeks, though the baby didn't shift under her hands, which was a concerning indication of vigour.

'She's not my first baby. This is my fourth. Four in five years.'

'Oh, my. Congratulations.' Faith's brows rose as she looked at the woman again. 'You look too young for four young kids. I have one and look much more careworn.'

Cynthia smiled wanly. 'John and I have just been on a week's holiday together. We were feeling relaxed.' She clutched her stomach again. 'I think this baby is wanting out.'

Faith narrowed her eyes and glanced at the clock. Only two minutes since the last contraction. 'Were there any complications in your previous births? Like a Caesarean or forceps. Or bleeding after the birth?'

'No. Apparently I'm made to have babies.'

Faith smiled. 'Pleased to hear it.' She listened to the clop of the baby's heart rate, which made the mother's mouth tilt up in relief at the comforting sound. Then Cynthia gasped, 'Oops. I think I just had a show or my waters broke a little. Something feels wet.'

By the time Faith had confirmed that there had been a small loss of blood and they'd sorted that development, Cynthia was returned to the sitting position. 'Um.' She fluttered her hands and her eyes darted around the room. 'I need John. I think I want to push.' Cynthia's voice sounded tremulous, alarmed at the speed of change, and Faith frowned and looked at the phone across the room just as the nurse poked her head into the room.

Faith blew out her breath in relief. 'Perfect timing. Can I have a delivery set-up ASAP? And get the supervisor to find out how far away Dr Southwell is. We need him now.' Faith didn't often call the doctor but this was a post-accident baby and it could be born compromised.

There was still that concern about abruption of the placenta from the sudden stop. 'Can you also ask Dr Salvanelli to stand outside the door in case I need to call him in, please, until the doctor arrives?'

The nurse nodded and hurried off after pulling the resus trolley closer to Faith.

Cynthia sighed heavily on the bed and Faith pulled back the sheet she'd lain over her. 'How about we just ditch the whole idea of underwear and check what's going on so we know for sure?'

By the time they'd done that Faith didn't need to check anything more because there was an unmistakable bulge of baby's crown inching into the world.

'I need to move,' Cynthia gasped. Already she was rolling onto her knees. Faith hurriedly stacked pillows so Cynthia could lean over a support. Things were progressing very quickly and the email of pre-birth papers would be moot until after baby's arrival now.

Faith leaned forward and pressed the call bell for the nurse to return. For now she needed an injection for after the birth so they didn't have a haemorrhage. Fourth baby made the risk increased. They could find out the medical history later.

Because the bag of waters was still intact, a large odd-shaped bag of fluid encased in membranes formed in front of the baby's head and through that a dark-haired skull could be seen descending. 'Looks like this baby wants to be born without breaking your waters first.'

'One of my others did that,' Cynthia panted. 'Won't drown, they said.'

Faith did love old wives' tales about midwifery, and even more she loved uncomplicated women like Cynthia who just went ahead and had their babies without any help from anyone.

'Come on, you,' Cynthia muttered as she bore down, because after progressing rapidly, with the birth of more of the head, now the speed of descent seemed to have stopped.

Faith glanced towards the door; it was

good knowing she did have backup help if needed, but she refrained from calling in Raimondo.

The nurse came back in carrying an injection tray. Faith smiled at her. 'Brownie points for you.' She nodded at the injection. 'Did you get onto Dr Southwell?' Faith's eyes returned to Cynthia, who had become more distressed.

'They had to find him but he's coming.'

Without looking at the nurse, Faith nodded. 'Great. Thanks.'

'It feels stuck. I need to move.' Faith wasn't surprised. But with a sore ankle, squatting would be hard.

'Would it be okay if I ask Dr Salvanelli to come in? He could take some of your weight as you try to get comfortable while the nurse sets up the rest of the equipment.'

'Do it.' Cynthia didn't have words to waste.

Faith raised her voice. 'Raimondo?'

Within seconds Raimondo stood beside her and between them they lowered the bed closer to the floor, helped Cynthia shift sideways on her knees until she was at the edge of the bed, and waited for the next contraction to ease before they moved further.

A minute later she stretched her left leg down towards the floor, then moaned and they all froze.

Cynthia sucked in a breath. 'That shifted a little. Let's go for a squat, which is how all my other babies were born.' Except this time her right leg wouldn't bear her weight.

Faith and Raimondo's eyes met across the woman's head. 'I always listen to the mother,' Faith said quietly and Raimondo nodded.

'I have you.' Raimondo's hands were under Cynthia's armpits. 'Stand and then you can release the weight.'

Cynthia shuffled sideways with Raimondo taking her full weight, not something Faith or the nurse could have done, and the woman sagged against him and bent her knees. She sighed with relief. 'Better. Much better.'

Faith took the warmed towel the nurse had handed her and wondered philosophically what would happen to Raimondo when the waters broke.

A sudden whoosh delivered the answer as the membranes overextended their elasticity and a wave of amniotic fluid hit the floor and bounced backwards, covering his shoes behind the mother in a hot wave of sticky fluid. Faith bit her lip to stop the smile, safe behind the towel and concentrating on what she hoped would happen next.

As expected, the baby's impacted shoulder that had held up the birth suddenly freed with the extra room in the pelvis from the squatting position, and baby slid into the warm towel Faith caught her with. A slithery cord-wrapped bundle who lay still.

'A girl,' Faith murmured.

The nurse, standing to the side of all the drama, reached over and clicked on the timer to begin recording time passed since birth.

Cynthia swayed and her face paled. 'I need to lie down.' Almost before she'd finished the words Raimondo had scooped her up and put her back against the pillows. The nurse stepped forward with a warm blanket to cover her and Faith juggled the still attached baby onto the edge of the mattress and dried the infant, waiting for the mewling to start.

At the end of the pulsating cord the silent baby didn't cry. Or move.

'Right then,' Faith said quietly as she clamped and cut the cord. 'I'm just going to take her to the trolley and check your baby out, Cynthia. I think she's stunned by the quick trip through the birth canal.'

The nurse took Faith's place beside the bed and patted Cynthia's shoulder. 'I'll take over here. We'll ask if I need any help. Here's a warm blanket as we wait for the afterbirth and your baby to come back. Let's get you comfortable while we wait.'

Raimondo followed Faith as she lifted the little towel-wrapped bundle onto the wheeled resuscitation bench and removed the damp cloth. She began to rub the baby with the new towel waiting under the overhead heater and Raimondo took the stethoscope that hung there and put it in his ears to listen to the baby's chest as soon as Faith finished.

With the lack of response she glanced at the ticking clock and reached for the little mask. 'Positive pressure ventilation at thirty seconds after birth.'

'Heart rate one-ten.' Raimondo stepped back as Faith slid the tiny clear breathing mask over the baby's mouth and nose. They watched the rise of the little chest as she began to puff small breaths of pressured air every second. Raimondo unwound the tiny pulse oximeter lead and strapped the sensor onto the pale baby hand. 'I'll get this running so we can tell how her oxygen levels are.'

'Good. Still think she's just stunned.' Faith turned her head towards the bed. 'Heart rate is good, Cynthia. She's just figuring out this breathing game.'

The nurse called out, 'And we've finished third stage over here and no bleeding after the placenta.'

That was a blessing. 'Thanks, Nurse.'

After thirty seconds of further inflations the tiny limbs began to move. Raimondo had calibrated the pulse oximeter and now the constant read-out of heart rate confirmed baby's heart was chugging along as it should but baby's breathing was still gasping and ineffectual, though Faith's maintenance of air entry stopped deterioration.

'I'll do another thirty seconds of air.' But Faith wasn't happy. Baby should have recovered by now. 'Can you have a look with a laryngoscope? Might be something that blocked the airway.'

Raimondo nodded and the tension in her shoulders increased as he took over the hand-held intermittent positive pressure ventilation for the baby while she assembled the equipment needed. Her hands collected the necessary equipment swiftly as her mind searched for reasons. Simple obstruction was the most likely cause for baby not breathing when the heart rate was so good but she was getting worried.

They didn't have sick babies often but this baby had been in an accident and was slightly premature.

Having Raimondo here beside her while she waited for the other doctor was surreal, wonderful in the circumstances, but probably not legal. Where was their backup?

She took the ventilation mask off Raimondo and he took the laryngoscope gently—angling the curved beak with a light at the end and peering down the baby's throat into the airways. She noted how skilfully he inserted the steel blade and narrowed his eyes at the now open and visible airway. 'A small blood clot obscuring the trachea—it must flop back when you stop forcing the air in.' He held out his hand, still focused on the airway. 'Sucker?'

Faith had the thin clear tubing ready and handed it to him to slide down the curve of the laryngoscope. His finger occluded the mechanism, they heard the gurgling sound of suction, then a dark clot slid up the tube and flashed past towards the vacuum bottle.

Raimondo removed the tube and the laryngoscope from the baby's throat in one smooth movement and Faith felt relief expand inside her. That skill was one she didn't have.

He smoothed the baby's forehead. 'Is this better?' he asked her.

The baby gasped and cried and Faith sagged a little with the rush of success and knew everything would be fine. Her eyes met Raimondo's in a moment of pure relief and satisfaction. 'Thank you,' she mouthed, and when he smiled at her the connection between them flooded all the way down to her toes.

CHAPTER SEVEN

RAIMONDO FELT THE link between them as if it were a physical bond drawing them closer. How was this so? He watched as Faith, after a last glance at him, turned away and carried the now wriggling baby across to the mother, and knew that his life would always hold this so precious memory of working with Faith.

A moment in time.

The beginning of a child's life.

A moment such as this he had missed at his own child's birth.

He jerked himself back to the present. It had been a simple thing to find the airway obstruction, but Faith's adeptness was also a reason for much satisfaction. He'd known she would be efficient and kind in her work but her calmness and competence during the rapid birth and the subsequent neonatal resuscitation made him feel a strange emotion he wasn't familiar with.

Was it pride? Approval that the mother of his daughter was so admirable? He thought about that. No. It was simple pleasure at helping Faith, at sharing a moment of release of tension, of mutual satisfaction and appreciation for the goodness of others. He was glad and thankful to be here for her. That was the emotion he felt. Gratitude.

But standing here now was not needed and impacted on the privacy of the patient. 'Congratulations, Cynthia. I will go out and try the ambulance control again for an update. Would you like me to pass the news on to your husband?'

The woman looked up. 'Yes. Please. I want to know how he is.'

As Raimondo walked down the hallway an elderly gentleman with a stethoscope around his neck, and a decided limp, hobbled past him towards the birthing unit. The doctor had arrived.

Raimondo didn't slow him with introductions.

By the time he had contacted ambulance control and ascertained the transport for Cynthia would be here soon, the nurse had returned to find out the results of his call. He passed them on and decided he would leave Faith to the no doubt mountain of paperwork she would have after such a rushed birth.

He would see her tomorrow. Today he needed to find himself a base in Lighthouse Bay because already he could tell he would always want to spend time here.

The next morning, just before eight, Raimondo strode up the cliff path towards a small house that sat to the left of the three crofts perched over Lighthouse Bay. He glanced back behind him to the soaring white stone lighthouse silhouetted against the sapphire-blue sky. The white tower seemed to watch him with guarded eyes from the big hill behind the hospital. Willing him to do this right.

So much at stake.

Perhaps even his whole future at stake.

Not just for Chloe, the daughter he had not known he was blessed with, but for Faith. For their future. His and Faith's future as parents together.

A week ago he had only a throwaway

comment from a colleague to suggest he had a child.

Twenty-four hours ago he had not known that inside his chest lay a switch that would illuminate the dormant fascination and feelings he still held for Faith. This woman who had borne his child alone yet forgiven his absence so that Chloe would not be soured by a mother's bitterness.

How had he stumbled on this rainbow of hope that could change his life? How did he not destroy his chance here, as he had so many times by taking the wrong path?

Faith had to see he could be trusted and would take as much care not to hurt their daughter as she would.

A stone flew away from the side of his boot and he slowed. He could have driven to Faith's house up the steeply inclined hill from the hospital but he'd preferred to walk to loosen the excited apprehension that had made him toss and turn for most of the night.

He'd run over and over the episode at the hospital and marvelled at the opportunity to see Faith in her work. She'd been as wonderful as he'd expected and the privilege of sharing those moments stayed with him.

Comforted him in his anxiety to do everything that was right by Faith.

He shook his head ruefully and smiled at the ancient front gate he approached. The new padlock.

There had been such a high from that shared medical emergency, and perhaps his soaring mood could have been partially responsible for his impulsive purchase of the building he was about to pass.

He turned his head and studied his new acquisition in the morning light: the run-down almost-mansion next door to Faith's home that he'd seen in the real estate window, walking home from the excitement at the hospital.

Still, the technicalities of purchasing something in a foreign country had taken his mind off his nervousness about meeting his daughter today. Perhaps if Chloe knew that her father had actually bought a house in her own town then she would feel more confident he was planning to be a part of her life. Faith would see this too. He hoped that was what she'd see.

But this morning the importance of this meeting with his new daughter had him edgy and unsettled. An unaccustomed apprehension that had not been helped even by rising at dawn and jogging down along the beach to freshen his mind. The cool white Australian sand under his bare feet had reminded him not at all of the hard pebbles of Amalfi beaches, his family holiday destination, and he felt the outsider even more despite his appreciation of the beauty surrounding him.

He'd jogged the sweeping inlet of Lighthouse Bay, the coarse sand curved like a new moon, and passed the rushing of the tide through the fish-filled creek back into the sea.

So few people passed him, strange for a man used to the crowds of Florence! So different to his homeland, but everything was different. His future was different because the occupants of this house he'd stopped outside now held his new world in their hands.

Now the moment had arrived his nerves were taut again and the day felt harshly warm against his skin already.

Or was he hot from nerves?

What if Faith had had a change of heart

overnight and decided to exclude him for some reason he could not fight?

What if his daughter cried when she saw him?

Would the father she had never met be a disappointment?

'Calm yourself, Raimondo,' he admonished out loud. His pocket held a small, traditionally dressed Italian doll, a whim he'd scooped up at the airport and had the clerk wrap in tissue paper for protection. The vivid red peasant apron and hat had caught his eye because the figurine had been exclaimed over by a passing young girl of around the same age as Chloe. Such a purchase might give the child he'd come to see a smile.

For that was what he wanted the most.

A smile from a little girl who could be such a shining light in his suddenly empty life—if she'd let him in.

If her mother let him. If he was invited into their world.

The door opened and Faith stood like a Renaissance vision of dark wavy hair and warm tanned skin, framed in the glow of sun that shone across from the windows overlooking the bay. He blinked and, incredibly, forgot for a moment his reason for being here. This woman, how she grabbed his chest and squeezed always.

'You look beautiful.' The words were soft and heartfelt and she stilled while her cheeks pinked.

'Thank you,' said politely like a schoolgirl, which reminded him abruptly about another girl. He had a daughter. *Madonna mia.* So much to take in.

While he still struggled she said, 'Thank you so much for yesterday.' Then she smiled. 'Both times.'

His mind flashed back to the old man and the new infant and the drama that followed the birth. 'You are very welcome.'

'Sorry about your shoes.' They smiled at each other.

'Nothing a shower and clean couldn't fix,' he demurred.

'Come in. I've told Chloe I have a friend from Italy coming this morning.'

Her words sank in and reality slapped him as his fogged brain cleared. The irrational disappointment of not being introduced as Chloe's father redirected his mind from the mother but he schooled his disappointment behind his professional mask.

Of course she would think this was better for the child, less pressure.

Later, he reassured himself, later they could change his title when all went well.

They would. Yes. A definite, not an 'if'.

But his heart sank as he was reminded that his position was precarious still and it wasn't this woman's fault he was the outsider.

His eyes roamed the room as he entered but he couldn't see Chloe.

A tall woman in her forties with Faith's dark hair in a blunt bob stood to one side, a calm expression in her green eyes as she watched him enter. He glimpsed a quickly suppressed smile and his nerves settled a little. No hostility here either, though he wasn't sure he deserved such generosity from the woman he assumed was Faith's aunt.

Faith gestured with her hand. 'Izzy? This is Raimondo. Raimondo, my aunt Isabel.'

'It's a pleasure to meet you, Raimondo.' She stepped forward and took his hand in both of hers. When she squeezed his fingers he felt the friendliness and lack of reserve her niece had projected from the first moment he'd met her.

An amazing family—and one he had let down so badly.

'And you. Thank you for your kindness, Isabel.' Instead of shaking her hand, he leaned forward and gently kissed both soft cheeks.

Then Faith moved from where she'd been blocking his view of Chloe, and finally he could see the child in the room.

His daughter.

There she was.

He could never mistake her for any but his own, though she had Faith's eyes.

'Mia cara bambina...'

The words were low and heartfelt. Except for the green eyes of her mother, she was his own dear *mamma*, a beauty as a young girl, judging from the photo he had in his home.

My darling child. Words failed him and inside his chest it felt as though someone squeezed his heart in warm hands. His Chloe was taller than he'd expected and more curious than he had hoped for as her little face tilted sideways and she examined him with interest.

He looked back at his daughter. She held out her hand as if she were a five-year-old queen. *'Buongiorno,'* she said with an Australian accent and he laughed.

'Buongiorno, piccolo.' He glanced at Faith and for an instant he saw what she had hidden behind her apparent serenity. The clenched hands of trepidation that he would hurt her child, the chewed lip of hope that he would be a good father for Chloe, and the bowed head of having to share her baby with another parent after all these years.

In a second he saw that and vowed he would protect the mother as well as the child from hurt.

Then Faith smiled, shaking her head at her daughter despite the worry in her eyes. He needed to remember this was so hard for her.

Faith nodded towards her daughter. 'Our one Italian word she practised for you.'

'Spoken perfectly,' he said gravely to Chloe with sincere hope he hadn't embarrassed her by laughing. 'You took me by surprise and I am very impressed. Thank you for learning the greeting.' His heart felt as if it were bursting. She was glorious and intelligent and had humour. And she looked like her beautiful mother. And somehow his. How had he been so blessed?

This was all due to his Faith.

'You're welcome,' she said primly and looked at her mother then back at him. 'Mummy says you're staying for breakfast and then we're going to the beach. We've made coffee in the coffee machine for you. I helped put the froth on top of the cup.'

'This is wonderful. Thank you.' Again his eyes were drawn to Faith, who seemed so remarkably calm, while his heart was pounding and his mouth was dry with excitement. He had a daughter.

He wondered at Faith's serenity then noted the repetitive reach for her necklace when she thought he wasn't looking. Perhaps not so calm.

He owed her so much for this meeting.

Inside he was wanting to shout with unexpected pride and joy and already the idea of leaving in less than a week caused pain that he would have to address and make plans for. Plans that meant his return. But that was for later. Today he would spend time with the daughter he had just found and try to mend bridges with the woman he had so badly disappointed.

Faith's aunt stepped forward. 'Would you like a pastry for breakfast?' She pointed to the dish of steaming croissants curled on the dish. 'There's butter and jam to go with it. We're having cereal and you can join us as well if you'd prefer.' She glanced around at the girls. 'Then we'll have a croissant to finish with too.'

'Grazie.'

'Before she came to live with us, Izzy travelled a fair bit,' Faith said. 'She says this is the only time of the day to drink cappuccino in Italy without being teased. Is that true?'

Raimondo smiled again. 'True. Milk is for morning *caffè*, and too heavy for the afternoon. And your croissants are perfect, Izzy. Thank you.'

They all stood there for an uncomfortable few seconds until Faith motioned them all to the table.

Again, she had taken control, Raimondo noted. This assertive woman was not how he remembered her, but then years had passed. She intrigued him even more, but then he too had aged. Matured.

He wondered if she noted that. Wondered if she thought of him like that at all. But this was not to be his concern. His concern was the young girl hopping from foot to foot as she tried to understand what was going on. This was about how he could become a part of Chloe's life to her benefit.

'Sit down, everyone. We'll eat then we'll go down to the beach for the morning.' Faith looked at her aunt. 'Have you decided if you're coming to the beach, Izzy?'

'I'll go up and see Myra. She's upset by her husband's fall yesterday.'

Faith turned to Raimondo. 'You would have seen Dr Southwell yesterday, as he came into the hospital limping?'

Raimondo nodded.

'He fell on the path on the way down to our emergency yesterday. He's okay but Myra is upset and worried. It's his second fall. She wants him to retire. They live in one of the crofts up higher.'

'Ah. I'm sorry to hear of his accident. I have seen those crofts. The view must be as good as from here.'

They all glanced towards the windows overlooking the road and the sea. All except his daughter, whose eyes he could feel on him.

'Even better. The ocean seems to go on for ever out of the windows.' He listened to Faith's answer though a part of him remained focused on his daughter. He turned and smiled at the child.

Chloe watched him as the conversation continued and finally she said diffidently, 'Excuse me. Would you like to try your coffee?' Obediently he lifted his cup. Her gaze followed the mug, watching him for his expression, her tiny pink mouth compressed in concentration.

He sipped and, though weak, the flavour tasted very pleasant. *'Perfetto,'* he said.

Her brows creased as she thought about that. 'Perfect?'

Pride expanded in him with an unfamiliar exuberance. 'See. You are a natural.'

CHAPTER EIGHT

A NATURAL? A natural what? A natural linguist?

Her daughter wasn't Italian.

Her daughter was a little Aussie through and through, Faith reassured herself as she remembered the stillness on his face and the blossoming wonder when he first saw Chloe.

And before that the moment when she'd said she'd introduce him as her friend not Chloe's dad. He'd looked gutted and for a moment she wished she could change that and erase his pain. Tell Chloe this man was her father and let Raimondo bask in the moment.

No. It was far too early to trust him not to illuminate their lives and then plunge them back into darkness.

Her brain whirled with each new direction the day was taking. Was it only yesterday Raimondo had reappeared? Her life lay scattered in unexpected directions like the sand down at the beach, covered after a storm with new treasures and new sadness. But they would sort it out. She would sort it out.

She guessed at some stage Chloe would travel to see the land her father came from. Whether or not Faith went along as well would depend on how old her daughter was when this hypothetical trip happened.

Stop. Faith drew a deep breath and sipped her coffee too fast and had to furtively wipe away the moustache that coated her lip. Cappuccino and croissants for breakfast. Good grief. These logistical issues were all Raimondo's problems, not hers.

She had her own many things to think about and the nebulous future was not as important as today would be.

Raimondo turned his head to answer a question from Izzy. Faith watched her daughter as Chloe gazed at the big Italian, her eyes wide and her attention settled squarely on this stranger at their table. True, it was an unusual sight to see a man in their feminine household. And true, Raimondo was difficult to tear your eyes away from.

Faith had thought that the first time she'd seen him at Sydney Airport—the young excited midwife returning to her little rural hospital after an exciting weekend birthing conference and then tangling gazes with the big handsome Italian man. The overhead announcement of flight delays drawing them together in mutual acceptance of the fickleness of fate.

Then, later, when he'd insisted on buying her dinner when their flights were rescheduled again to an even later flight. The instant, compelling attraction that had leapt between them growing bigger and brighter like a flame the more time they'd spent together. A flame that had taken over all good sense on both sides so that when the flights had been put back again until the next day they'd ended up in her hotel room provided by the airline instead of each to their own room later that night.

The next morning, with stars in their eyes, instead of going their separate ways, he'd followed her home to see this place she loved so much and they'd spent every minute together until the fateful phone call that had torn them apart.

That moment when the magical, marvellous moments had ended abruptly.

With an almost brutal finality.

Raimondo turned back and caught her haunted expression. Yes, I'm shell-shocked, she thought, and wished she could say it out loud. Just like I was years ago, and I don't know why I was destined to meet you like this twice in my lifetime. Not fair, really.

But she would have to deal with the moment and trust that he was trying to right a wrong and not cause more trouble.

What did he expect of her? Of Chloe? And what was the best way to keep her and Chloe safe from falling under his spell again and being hurt? That was what she needed to know. The order of her world seemed to have been snatched from beneath her feet yesterday, but hopefully it would return to how it had been.

Almost six years since she'd been swept along on a wild ride that culminated with the birth of this pretty, dark-haired child who brightened her life with such joy. What would it mean to share her with Raimondo—for that was what she could see coming? Maybe it would be for the best as Chloe did miss having a dad she could at least picture in her mind.

What was not for the best was to risk her own heart falling for the same attraction that had skittled her life last time.

Mentally she checked her defences and they were in place. She would see how the day panned out and make sure she too stayed safe.

An hour later the three of them walked down the hill to the beach.

Chloe was dressed head to foot in a delightful blue-striped rash shirt, frilled tights and matching soft peaked sunhat. The only parts of her that could be burnt were her face, hands and feet and Faith had sunscreened them. They spent so much time at the beach the covering swimwear was easier than catching Chloe for the trauma of sunscreen, which she hated.

For herself she wore a long sleeve cotton shirt and took it off to swim only. It was disquietingly odd to be going on a 'family' outing with Raimondo and her daughter, even if Chloe didn't know that was what it was.

The path swung in narrowly beside the

road and Faith chose to follow behind the other two as it gave her time to think, and she could catch snatches of conversation as they floated back. Though, walking behind him, it did draw her eyes to the taut definition of his muscular arm as he swung the basket and the shift of thick muscles on his shoulders through his thin white shirt.

She'd loaded Raimondo with the two folding chairs and the not-feather-light food basket and he'd very happily accepted them. *His arms will have grown by the time he gets there*, she thought with an amused acknowledgement—it was easy to picnic when he carried most of the stuff. Faith carried the umbrella, towels and a blanket and Chloe swung her bucket and spade.

Chloe was saying, 'The beach has a low and a high tide and you have to be careful when you walk on the rocks when the tide's coming in.'

Her daughter definitely wasn't fazed, talking to this big Italian her mother said was a friend.

'Thank you for the warning. I will be careful,' Raimondo assured her.

A small arm pointed to the opposite cliff. 'That lighthouse is so the ships know that the land is there. Especially in a storm. Aunty Trina's house has big windows and in the storm the wind howls.'

A sage nod from Raimondo. 'That must be very exciting in a storm.'

'I don't like storms,' Chloe said severely, and Faith had to smile as Raimondo backtracked adroitly.

'Neither do I.'

Chloe looked at him under her brows as if assessing his truthfulness and Faith suppressed a laugh.

As if reassured, Chloe went on. 'Mummy works at the hospital on the hill and I'll be going to big school next year, which is just down the road from the hospital.' Her daughter could talk.

Faith could also be amused by how mystified Raimondo looked by Chloe's running commentary because he kept turning back to Faith and smiling in pleased bemusement and she suspected he hadn't had much to do with children.

Well, Faith had had a lot to do with children. Especially this one. Twenty-four hours a day and seven days a week for almost five years and still Chloe could stump her.

He had no chance of nailing it on one brief week-long visit.

Chloe had always been included in the conversations between Faith and Izzy and, while a very polite little girl, she was happy to share her views on the small world she inhabited.

No doubt, soon Chloe would ask Raimondo about his town and his life so that he could share things with them—things that she had no knowledge of. Her daughter was thirsty for knowledge of new things. New places. There were certainly opportunities coming up for her there. For Faith too.

Crossing her fingers, Faith hoped her daughter could wait for those questions until they reached the beach so she could hear the answers too.

'The book Mummy is reading me at the moment is called *Chicken Little*. Have you read it?'

Faith smiled to herself at Raimondo's answer. 'No. What is this story about?'

Chloe turned her head to look at him. Faith suspected her daughter rolled her eyes at that point. 'A silly chicken thinks the sky is falling and tells all the animals they have to leave. To run. It's very funny.'

'I am glad that it is funny.' Raimondo turned slightly to look at Faith for an instant. 'Perhaps your mummy could read that story to you again, and I could listen?'

Chloe stopped and turned back to Faith. 'Mummy? Could you read the *Chicken Little* story when Mr Salvanelli comes to visit?'

Faith shooed her on. 'We'll see.'

'So is Italy bigger than Lighthouse Bay?' Chloe's question came as his daughter settled down again on the sand. They were on the beach and had made a small area their own with their things.

Raimondo liked that there was nobody else here. So strange when it was such a picturesque spot, but perhaps more families would come later.

The chairs Faith had given him to bring were set up and the umbrella she'd carried angled over them all. His daughter played at their feet with a small bucket and spade in the sand and he felt like pinching himself to be sure he wasn't dreaming this moment in time.

He was with his family.

Every now and then his daughter would

run on sturdy legs to the water's edge and fill her bucket with water and bring it back to pour over sand so she could plaster the walls of the mound she said was a castle.

It began to take shape. He'd never made a sandcastle as a boy but could see the attraction. Perhaps he could try? To help her. Chloe began to stick shells on the walls. He glanced at Faith but she was staring out over the sea, deep in thought.

'May I join you?' he asked Chloe.

Chloe nodded vigorously. 'We can make it taller.'

So, awkwardly, for he had no skills with children, he crouched down on the sand beside his daughter and began to scoop out the sand in a narrow line to build a moat, putting the sand he removed on the top of her mound. The sand was cool and damp and coarse and felt strangely comforting as he ran his fingers across its salty cleanness to smooth the new walls of the castle.

'I see you build good castles. I am a man. We build forts. So, with your permission, I will dig a moat and build a wall to keep our castle safe from those who might attack while you make it pretty.' Was he being too stereotypical?

She laughed. 'The water will attack it.'

'I will build a diversion for the water.'

Each time she patted on another handful of sand it was as if she had also found a question. He had to smile at her fertile and free-flowing mind.

He had hundreds of questions and couldn't seem to ask any.

So instead he thought how to describe his home when she asked about it. 'I live on the outskirts of the city of Florence. It is much bigger than Lighthouse Bay.' He thought about his beautiful Florence and the thousands of people who lived there and the hundreds who visited every day. Unlike this tiny place. 'Our house is part of a very old villa belonging to a nobleman many years ago but purchased by my grandfather and restored. It has several buildings and many rooms and a garden that grows olives and looks over Florence and the Arno Valley.'

He saw Faith look up at that. She raised her brows at him with shock in her eyes but he pretended not to see. They had not spoken of Italy much in the time they'd spent together.

'How many rooms?' His daughter remained persistent.

'There are four other dwellings but the main house has ten bedrooms.' He shrugged. 'My brother's house has nine bedrooms. Mine has six.'

'That sounds big.' Here she looked at her mother. 'That's big, isn't it, Mummy?'

Faith looked at her daughter. 'Sounds a bit like the size of the hospital, really,' she said, her voice dry. 'You know how it has some separate buildings with other wards in them. Instead of looking over the ocean, his house looks over a city and a valley.'

His daughter nodded and looked much struck. 'You must have a big family.'

He spread his hands. 'And this is our sadness.' He shrugged. 'No. My twin lost his wife and son and I am not married any more. We are the last of our family.'

Chloe lowered her brows and shook her head, her little face serious. 'You should get married and have a family.'

'Yes, I should.' He glanced ruefully at Faith. 'My brother and I both should marry but his love died and mine wasn't meant to be.'

He saw Faith turn away to hide her expression, or to look at something he could not see. He wished she had not turned her face. Then she turned back and there was something in her face that made him pause in his explanation.

Faith said quietly, 'It's not polite for little girls to tell adults what they should do, Chloe.'

'Oh?' She glanced at her mother and sighed. 'Okay. Sorry, Mr Salvanelli.'

Just like that. No angst from either, just a correction. Different to his upbringing, where the emotion always ran high and even the wrath of God was often introduced. So different. He searched for a way to reassure both. 'I am not offended but thank you for your apology. I have a question. Do you always make sandcastles or do you make other things in the sand?'

The change of topic was gratefully accepted by all parties.

'I make sandcastles, though they're not really castles. I've never seen a castle except in books about princesses. I love princesses.'

She could certainly hold a conversation. He was glad English was his second language and he didn't have to translate in his thoughts. She was adorable and he couldn't help considering how his family home was very much like a castle.

He would show her one day, hopefully not too far away in time, and with luck she would be enchanted. But that possibility remained with her mother, who was watching him with an inscrutable expression on her beautiful face. Inside himself he knew that he would also like to show Faith his world, but at the moment that look on her face warned him to be careful.

'Mummy said you are a doctor?'

His eyes returned to his daughter. 'Yes, I work in a part of Florence that is poor and the people come to our clinic because it is free. Sometimes I work in other countries if there is a disaster.' Though he couldn't get away as much as he liked since his brother's wife had died.

'Mummy is a midwife.'

'I know. I saw her at her work yesterday.'

'Do you catch babies too?'

This he didn't understand. 'Catch babies?' He looked at Faith. 'Babies who fall?'

When Faith laughed her mouth curved with amusement, her eyes crinkled and the already ridiculously bright day seemed to grow sunnier to him.

She explained, 'In the past it was said that the doctor "delivered" the baby. Of course, it is the mother who does all the work so here we say we are only there to ensure the safe gathering of the mother's work. So to "catch a baby" as it is born. Chloe has heard me say it many times.'

He smiled at his daughter. 'Yes. Rarely I catch babies but mostly I help those who are sick. Little girls and boys your age. Old ladies and men who are frail. I have come to know many families from the outskirts and it is something I am proud of.'

Chloe was so interested in him. Thirsty for knowledge he could share. He was having a wonderful conversation with his daughter!

For a moment he so deeply regretted the lost time. Maria had a lot to answer for by keeping this news from him… He could feel his mood slipping and Faith's calmness seemed to wrap around him as he considered who really had suffered.

That was not all Maria's doing and bitterness would taint this new promise of a family. He would not do that. No. This was his doing and he would be the one to repair any damage. He had been the one who had flown from Australia into his family's turmoil, into deathbed promises to a man he owed everything, and into funerals. He had been distracted but had not once paused to check, to confirm the safety or check for unexpected complications from his incredible but reckless Australian liaison.

It did not matter that he'd had a marriage to arrange. Then a funeral.

Years he had wasted.

But at the time he'd thought they hadn't been reckless. He had used protection and she also. The thought of this accident of birth occurring sixteen thousand kilometres away had never occurred to him.

It should have occurred to confirm Faith's wellbeing though.

And after Maria had left? Why had he accepted that Faith was in his past and would be settled happily without him? Why had he assumed their amazing connection had meant so little to her when its magic had settled in a space in his heart that it would never leave?

He'd been determined to fill his life with work when he should have returned at least once to Australia to confirm she was happily settled and his own thoughts were the only ones wistful for what had ended. He still didn't know the answer to that question but had yet to be convinced there wasn't hope.

The time after divorcing Maria he hadn't wasted, because he'd given it to others. It had been healing to draw strength from those in poverty wearing quiet fortitude so that he could not feel sorry for himself. Both locally and abroad in disaster zones.

Helping others after the dissolution of his marriage, and the tragic loss of his brother's family, he'd found peace from unobtrusively being present in their need.

But he'd wasted his chance of happiness.

Wasted Faith's chance of happiness.

Wasted time he could have spent with Chloe.

But now he would work towards the challenge of proving himself worthy of Faith and Chloe. This was his new goal for a future that stretched ahead. He stared out over the white sand, over the tumbling shallows, over the rolling waves to the place where the ocean met the sky and prayed that he could be worthy to become a part of their lives.

CHAPTER NINE

FAITH COULDN'T HELP responding to the depth in Raimondo's voice when he told Chloe about his practice in Florence and his aid work, though she knew his simple version was watered down for young ears.

Somewhere inside her a warm gladness expanded that he'd found a vocation he'd been lacking before. None of this passion had been there when he'd spoken of the business side of the pharmaceutical company. It had all been her enthusiasm for her work.

So now she was glad for him. Glad he'd found a purpose in life, even if he hadn't found a happy marriage.

But that didn't change anything. He hadn't looked back to what they'd had in those magical few days. If she let him into their lives now, and she couldn't see how she had a choice about that, it was going to be hard to trust him not to fly in like a comet until Chloe was starry-eyed and then zoom away again.

Certainly she would guard her own heart from him this time.

Looking back, she could see so clearly, his tilted head, his warm eyes as she'd raved about why she loved her job in maternity. He'd watched her as if she'd been the most beautiful, interesting woman he'd ever seen and she, young that she'd been, had been flattered and eager to expound her beliefs.

She even remembered that next day, taking him through the cave, raving about the way water seeped through limestone and dissolved the rocks to form caves. How wonderful it was.

He'd surely known that but she'd been too besotted not to spout all the things that inspired her in her cave tours and dragging him down to the ancient riverbed had seemed the best gift she could give him for the gift he'd given her—a whole new world of wonderful love, sensuality and awareness.

Which, sadly, had ended when he flew away for good.

The warmth in her belly abruptly changed to a chill.

Yes.

Be careful.

And be careful of Chloe falling in love too.

She glanced at her waterproof watch and recognised the sudden need to cool down. She struggled inelegantly out of her beach chair. 'Enough time has passed since breakfast. I think I'll go for a swim. Would you like to come and splash with me, Chloe?'

Her daughter jumped up immediately. 'Are you coming, Mr Salvanelli?'

Faith noted Raimondo's grimace at Chloe's formal address and, yes, she could see this was hard for him. But some of the softening she'd been unaware of had already caught her out.

She needed to stay vigilant and firm on boundaries between him and Chloe until she knew what he hoped for.

He might become the perfect dad.

Or not.

But she wasn't creating storybook fantasies of what daddies were like and wouldn't risk breaking Chloe's heart until she was sure the devotion would be reciprocated. For all she knew, he could be called away again tomorrow and off he'd go to answer a summons without a backward glance at them.

He had the right to leave any time.

She had the responsibility to protect her daughter in case he did.

'*Sí*, I will come.' He rose, a smooth uncoiling of muscles, and she dragged her eyes away from the leashed power of him. Darn him. How could getting out of a folding chair seem sexy? She turned away.

Then he said, 'Are you sure you do not need help with suncream on your back, Faith?'

The body part in question was directed to him so he couldn't see her eyes close as she imagined that. Big hands. Powerful fingers with slow movements. Sigh. Sensible was so darn sucky. 'No, I'm fine, thanks, I'll only be in and out of the water.'

She pushed herself forward through the sand, Chloe hopping beside her, as she headed for the sea. She needed to be clear on the boundaries for herself too.

They stayed at the beach for the morning, picking through the basket for food and drinks, choosing topics that sat easily as well, while the solitude of the beach slowly disappeared. Two surfers arrived and ran out into the waves. A lone fisherman walked the beach edge further along the bay.

Soon more families arrived, just as they were packing up. Ellie and her husband and daughter. The new arrivals dumped their chairs and towels beside them to greet them.

'Hello, people. Nice to see you.' Faith had relaxed enough for this to be almost true. Though she did wonder if Ellie had told Sam that Raimondo was Chloe's father. And what they all thought about Raimondo helping in maternity. At least she'd told Ellie about Raimondo.

It was actually neat that she could introduce him to the Southwells after the years of them knowing he'd been briefly in her past. 'This is Dr Raimondo Salvanelli from Florence. Raimondo, this is Ellie, my boss, and her husband, Dr Sam Southwell, and their daughter Emily.'

'Good to meet you, Raimondo,' Ellie said. 'I'm more the paper pusher than Faith's boss. We're self-directed here. Heard you two have been busy already.'

Faith thought of the birth yesterday, and then remembered the man who had collapsed. She needed to phone and find out how he was, but he'd been swept from her mind by Raimondo. How awful.

Raimondo must have read her thoughts. 'He was improving this morning when I rang.' Thank you, she thought silently.

Ellie had carried on. 'Congratulations on the successful resuscitation. Both of them. Faith was lucky you were there.'

Raimondo nodded a friendly greeting. 'Your midwife had it under control. Very nice to meet you both. Faith has mentioned you, Ellie. All good things,' Raimondo said, smiling, and his ease of manner made Faith's jangled nerves settle as he held out his hand to meet Sam's.

'Welcome to Lighthouse Bay,' Sam said. 'This your first time here?'

Raimondo smiled blandly. 'Second. I couldn't believe how deserted the beach was this morning. It is very different to Italy.'

Another family group hailed them. Catrina, another of the midwives and only recently on maternity leave, a month before her baby was due, waddled a little with the weight of her pregnancy. Her husband Finn arrived with his daughter Piper, who'd not long ago turned three, and two chairs. The little girls whooped and ran in circles, excited to see each other, and all the mothers smiled.

Introductions continued as Finn and Raimondo shook hands.

'You should join us for dinner tonight,' Ellie said. 'It's Sam's dad's birthday, and we're having a barbecue. Chloe would be excited to see the girls as well.'

'Who's working?' Trina asked as she shook hands with Raimondo.

'Broni. It's her last shift before holidays and then we have Stacey back from the base hospital.'

Faith, Raimondo and Chloe left the beach a few minutes later, having agreed to meet everyone for the barbecue, and wandered back up the hill with chairs, umbrella, a much lighter basket and a tired little girl with a bucket and spade bringing up the rear.

Faith struggled with herself on whether to invite Raimondo in as they neared the house. Did he need some time to himself? She guessed it had been a pretty big twenty-four hours.

The thought made her almost laugh out loud.

Here she was being a coward at the

thought of inviting him in. Scared to be alone with him because Chloe would probably go to sleep for an hour, something she'd been doing lately in the afternoon, and she did need to find out what Raimondo's plans were.

Perhaps better to search for answers, even if he was not ready for more time with her.

She looked across at him. 'Would you like to spend the afternoon with us, though Chloe will probably have a rest now, or are you jet-lagged and want to come back later before the barbecue?'

'Thank you, Faith.' He shook his head. 'Again, you surprise me with your kindness. And yes, please. I would like to talk with you this afternoon.'

She looked at this tall, handsome, serious man outside her door and tried again to think of this from his point of view. 'I don't think I'm being kind. Just practical.' She lowered her voice. 'We need to discuss things.'

She opened the gate, walked to the door and pushed it open.

When she looked back to invite him in his face had paled. 'You do not lock your door?'

She glanced back at the wooden door

she'd pushed open off the latch. 'Only if we go away. And that's more to stop it blowing open.' She watched Chloe put her sand bucket down wearily outside the door and kick off her sandy flip-flops. Faith brushed her daughter's dark hair with her hand as the little girl passed in front of them. 'Straight through into the bathroom, Missy.'

She turned back to watch Raimondo remove his beach shoes, trying to ignore the way his broad back rippled and his dark hair curled on his strong neck. Shook her head at herself. 'Come in when you're ready. I'll just get Chloe showered and she'll have a lie down and rest.'

She followed her daughter in but a subtle, sensitive part of her was very aware of the man following. 'There's an album on the table of Chloe's baby photos if you'd like to look at that while I sort Chloe out.'

His face lit when he saw the album she'd discreetly placed this morning before they left.

'Thank you.' Then a quirked brow in her direction and a slight smile. 'And after Chloe will you sort me out?'

She met his eyes. 'That's my plan.'

CHAPTER TEN

WHEN RAIMONDO LOOKED at his watch only fifteen minutes had passed since Faith had left him. Yet his daughter's whole life had passed before his eyes.

His chin felt raw where he'd continually rubbed in deep emotion with his chest tight and painful as he'd slowly turned the pages of his daughter's, and the beautiful Faith's, world.

A life he'd known nothing of while he'd passed his time on the other side of the planet, missing it all completely.

In his mind that first album page still haunted him and he could have wept for the loss for himself and for his Australian family. Could have wept for what might have been if he had known of Faith's pregnancy and Chloe's impending arrival.

Faith had done this alone.

Though no, not alone, for her aunt had been there. He and his family owed an enormous debt to Faith's aunt Isabel.

But he should have been the one to support the mother of his child.

He turned the pages back to the start, not for the first time, and gazed again. A rosy-skinned and radiantly exultant Faith, so young and so smiling up at the camera from a large circular bath, water lapping the swell of her breasts, and a little higher on her chest lay his brand-new owl-eyed baby daughter, staring into her mother's eyes, her tiny body slightly blue, patches of white vernix from the pregnancy still covering her plump baby creases as another woman leaned across to lay a towel over them both.

Dios. His heart actually felt as if it grew and expanded inside him and would explode out of his ribs, tearing his chest apart.

He turned forward the pages to the photos of his daughter's last birthday. The starfish cake, four candles, her baby face maturing into a bigger little girl, her mother's loving smile as she leaned across towards her daughter and helped blow out the candles. Such a moment, captured with love from the photographer. *Sì*, he owed Izzy a great debt. So many wonderful moments to be shared with him even as a future observer.

He heard Faith close the door gently to his daughter's room and then cross the lounge area towards him. Her bare feet whispered on the rugs that covered the wooden floors in circles of bright colour.

Her home radiated the same welcoming charm the woman did.

He looked down at the album and then towards her. Words failed him.

She brushed his shoulder in a fleeting touch of sympathy as she passed to sit opposite. 'You look…upset.' She was giving comfort to him when it should have been the other way around.

'Regretful.' He moistened his tight throat. 'The photographs are very beautiful.' Thankfully his voice remained steady. He pushed the album towards her chair when in fact he wanted to tuck it under his arm and run with it. 'Thank you for showing me.'

She straightened the big album on the table without opening the cover. 'Chloe looks at the photographs a lot.'

He laughed and even he could hear the exasperation. 'As would I. The photographer is gifted.'

'Izzy, of course. She's been good with everything.'

'I can see that I let you down.' Then he leaned forward. The silence stretched between them as he tried to form the words he needed. 'I don't understand. I never dreamed… How did this happen?

'Bah.' He waved his hand at the past, at his ludicrous statement. 'We know how…' And for a brief moment their eyes met and humour danced between them. Then it was gone.

'How do I ask this?' He ran his hand through his hair, anxious not to place blame because that would do neither of them good. 'I am sure we were exuberant, young and excited for this thing that sprang so powerfully between us…' he looked at her and the faint blush on her cheeks only made her more painfully beautiful '…but I thought we were careful?'

'It's a fair question…' she smiled ruefully '…and one I continually asked myself when that pregnancy stick proved positive.' She shrugged. 'We were careful.' Yet he could see she was embarrassed.

Her, embarrassed? A joke. Nothing she could do was anywhere near the moral catastrophe he had achieved and left her to deal with.

'I missed two pills during the conference before we met, though took them when we were together. So must have been susceptible to ovulate.' Her voice lowered. 'Apparently, we had needed that second defence. But by the time I found out it was too late as I was pregnant.'

He thought about that.

Thought about the lovely young woman he'd fallen for in the airport, fresh and vibrant. Almost innocent. So full of life and passion and enthusiasm for her work—and he had left her pregnant and with the heartbreak he'd caused her.

He could have destroyed her with his carelessness if she hadn't been so resilient. He thought about what he'd done to her ordered life and then he'd flown away without a backward glance. No. Even that hadn't been true.

He'd glanced back a lot. But those few days he had shared with Faith had been dreamlike. A mirage. Something he didn't deserve.

As if she'd read his mind she said softly,

'Maybe it's different for men. I'd like to know how you felt as you flew away.'

He owed her that.

Though he wondered if he could be as honest as she was. Regardless, he needed to be. Such a small price to pay. 'What you gave me in those few days was a gift and I cherished the memories in the months and years ahead. Yet it was strange how little I felt I deserved such happiness. Perhaps that is why I did not make it back. Wedding Marie was a return to the time of my grandfather. Without joy. But my duty. You were the dream I didn't deserve.'

He shrugged. 'Melodramatic, perhaps. You have to understand my family to understand my actions. But, even for my family, I would never have left you to face that alone. I never thought I would leave you pregnant.'

Faith recognised the sincerity. She hadn't imagined a child either or she would have asked for a morning after pill when she'd recovered from Raimondo's departure.

Thank goodness she hadn't or she wouldn't have her darling Chloe.

But Chloe was now a part of Raimondo's family and she'd better at least try to understand the Salvanellis to help her daughter when her time came to meet them.

'Tell me about your family.'

He looked struck by the suggestion. Then he said softly with wry humour as he held her gaze, 'Chloe's other family?'

'So it seems,' she said and tried to ignore the fission of fear that raised the hairs on her arms.

'One day.' No. She wouldn't lose her daughter to them as she had lost Raimondo when his family demanded his return. Nobody could demand Chloe did anything. 'But I do want to know why you didn't feel as if you deserved the happiness we so briefly found together.' They hadn't spoken of his family much at all back then.

'It is fair that you know of my family. Where to begin? Dominico, my brother, is ten minutes older, and with me was sent to live with our grandfather after the loss of our parents. That loss left nothing to soften the already stern man who was my *nonno*. Like our father before us, we studied medicine, despite a lack of enthusiasm from our grandfather, because neither of us had a passion for the business he loved. My brother took over the running of the business when my grandfather became ill. I am grateful to him for that.'

There was a lot there he wasn't saying but she got the general idea. Not the ideal childhood but she'd had loss in her life too, even though it had been later. 'No grandmother on the scene?'

'Gone at my father's birth. Our grandfather's estate was a loveless home, despite the beauty of Florence. Though that altered when Dominico found Teresa.'

She watched his face transform and had a sudden wish that she could have met this Teresa.

'Teresa brought joy,' Raimondo went on, but there was sadness in his voice. 'Soon their son arrived to liven their villa. Finally, my grandfather could relax, my brother was happy, I could stop feeling guilty that I was still furthering my career in medicine and not marrying. Now the family business was secure with two generations of sons to pass it down to.'

'Your brother and his wife were happy?'

'Indeed. Too brief happiness. Again, tragedy struck. We are not blessed with luck.' He stopped for a moment and she saw the shadow of that time as it passed through his mind.

'Not long before I came to Australia for business meetings, and met you, Teresa and my brother's son were killed in a hot-air balloon ride. Broken, my brother withdrew from everyone. I had to travel for the business—the Sydney trip already had been arranged—and suddenly it was back to me to ensure the line when my grandfather became terminally ill. But first I needed to complete the trip to Australia my brother wanted to cancel.'

'And you met me.'

'Sì.' His voice dropped and she almost missed the words as he spoke them more to himself. 'My Australian wildflower.'

She remembered he'd called her that. Faith felt the sting behind her eyes, the tightness in her throat, and chewed the inside of her top lip as she struggled to push it all back. This was too important to lose in an emotional blowout. One she'd dealt with years ago and locked securely behind iron gates inside her soul.

Hopefully he missed her struggle as he looked within himself to the painful past. 'You must understand my grandfather's whole world was centred on the pharmaceutical company he'd built. That it must stay in the Salvanelli family. Now, suddenly, my grandfather had days to live. My brother struggled with his demands and called me to come at once—so I went.'

She remembered his sudden departure. The first available flight arranged. The rush.

He looked up and sighed. 'The marriage between Maria and I had been spoken of for a long time and I had resisted. Both my promised wife and I had opposed the match. But my grandfather had so little time, and her father agreed, and it was either I wed the woman he wished or my brother could be persuaded into wedding Maria, and there was no marriage he could face, still grieving for his wife and son. I could feel his pain and would not ask it of him.'

Tough love. She could see his dilemma. And even why he hadn't explained the whole of it when he'd left.

But that was almost six years ago and he'd been free for a while. If she'd been his Australian wildflower, why hadn't he come back to see if what they'd had been real when he had the chance?

She quashed that bitterness. Needed to remember she had let it go a long while past.

But she couldn't help wondering what would happen if his brother called again. She wouldn't be stupid enough to expect him not to go instantly if he needed him, but what if Chloe was the one left heartbroken—what then?

'You didn't think to come back when the marriage was annulled?'

His heavy sigh lowered his shoulders until he straightened and faced her. 'Who was I to ruin your life again? I had no doubt you would have moved on without me. What we had was a few days on the other side of the world and you were young and not bitter with life like I had become.'

That was true. She had moved on. And she hadn't become bitter. Just thankful for her daughter and occasionally nostalgic for a man who could have been a big part of her life but had told her he would never be back.

She'd made the break he'd told her was permanent.

Raimondo went on. 'I believed you were better without me. Vibrant and passionate about your work. You gave me that. After Maria left I found an area in my work that brought me great satisfaction.' He met her gaze and held it. 'Until someone spoke of you, and your Lighthouse Bay…' a pause '…and your daughter—and suddenly there was nothing that was more important than coming here to see.'

At least the mention of the Bay had jogged him at last. He'd remembered them. 'And here you are.' There was no mistaking the hint of dryness in her tone.

'*Sì*. Here I am.'

Yes. Here stood the major concern. He was very capable of wreaking more havoc. She'd only have to remember the response her body made when he was near. Let alone if he turned the full force of his Italian gallantry and accomplishments her way. Plus, she suspected he had a depth of purpose and strong will he wasn't showing her.

Well, she had that too.

She lifted her head. 'Did you come with plans, Raimondo?'

She watched him blink at her direct question. 'If you are here for Chloe's birthday, are you leaving, never to come back again after this week?'

She shrugged as if unable to know what to believe, but all the time her eyes remained on his. 'No evasion, please. Is she to look for Christmas and birthday cards? Or are you hoping for more?'

He stared at her.

Well he might, but she was deadly serious.

Black widow serious.

She would protect her daughter from his charm if necessary. To the death. Nothing in his explanation said he wouldn't leave them suddenly if called.

Now, while Chloe was asleep, they needed to get this sorted and labelled for what it was.

'I understand your concern. You have become a strong woman, Faith.'

Pointless flattery. 'I've needed to be.'

'I have never lied to you.'

Bully for him. 'I've never lied either.' She raised one brow. 'So don't lie now.'

His turn to lift his chin and she saw the narrowing of his eyes, the implacable set to his chin, and now she could see the man he'd become. Perhaps he wouldn't run to do his family's bidding quite so quickly this time, but she wasn't sorry she'd pulled the tiger's tail.

Hopefully she hadn't set in motion the

whole attack mode response but he needed to know she was on her guard.

He leaned forward and it was as if he'd flipped a switch because in his eyes shone the force of his personality she'd suspected might be shaded.

Whoa.

Where had he been concealing this man?

His dark eyes glittered and his sensual mouth flattened into a straight line. 'Yes, I have plans. I did not come with them but after seeing you at the cave yesterday, hearing your story, I lay awake and dreamed of the future. Of what could be. Of the possibilities before all of us.

'Not just showing my daughter her Italian family and the world she needs to be now aware of.' His voice was deep. Clipped. Belying the fierce emotion in his eyes. 'I will do what needs to be done to achieve that dream. And other dreams.'

A little more of the strong guy than she needed. But she'd dealt with stressed dads before in the labour ward and she knew where she was going with this. Her end goal. 'Without pain to Chloe?'

He looked at her and then, miraculously, his eyes softened. Even held a glint of admiration. 'Correct. I agree. She is the most important part of the equation.'

'Thank you. More important than you. More important than me.' She sat back and he followed suit. 'That was the point I was trying to make.'

He measured her with an assessing look. 'I can see that now. I will not underestimate you again.'

Well, that wasn't quite what she'd been hoping for but she might as well get the answers she needed.

'And your immediate plans?'

He blew out his breath but in his eyes there was a definite admiration for her. The glint of a smile. The hint of a challenge. 'Three things. I would like to be here for Chloe's birthday. Be a part of her celebration.'

She nodded. That was easy. She'd already agreed.

'I would like to be allowed to buy her a gift.'

Again, Faith nodded. Chloe would be happy with that. And she was only five so he couldn't spend too much on her. 'As long as you don't buy her a house, the gift is fine.'

To her surprise he laughed out loud. 'That house has bolted.'

She blinked. 'It's "That horse has bolted".' The second time Raimondo had mistaken his metaphors. He didn't appear any less amused when she corrected him. Suspicion and disbelief raised the hairs on her arms. 'What do you mean?'

'In this case, I have bought a house, and the gate is bolted.' He grinned a wicked flash of white teeth at her. 'We are off topic and Chloe will wake soon, I imagine.'

Faith glanced at her watch but her head still spun at the assertive man she had definitely underestimated.

No. He did not just say that. 'Bull. When did you have time to do something that complicated?'

Dark brows arched at her. 'It is not complicated if others do the paperwork. Did you not spend eight hours at your place of work yesterday?' He spread his hands in a very Italian gesture. 'I am a rich man. I saw something I liked and it is done. But I can wait to put it in Chloe's name if you prefer.'

That was scary. He had done it. Bought a house for a five-year-old.

Or for himself to have access to Chloe.

On his first day back and before meeting her daughter. His actions defied sense.

'What house did you buy?' She guessed that meant he wasn't planning on never seeing Chloe again. She'd wanted that reassurance, hadn't she? But with this new broadside she didn't feel as confident she had everything under control.

He settled back and studied her. 'Which house do you think I would buy? Which house would be useful to me?'

She could feel her own temper slipping and knowing that he was goading her because she'd goaded him didn't help. 'Well, you can't buy mine because I own it.'

He waved the comment away. 'The one beside you. It is nothing. Me dealing with inactivity.'

Next door? Which house was for sale? Only one. The old Sea Captain's house. With the turrets. It was a wreck. She shook off the wild thoughts and concentrated. He had her off balance. That wasn't good. He'd just bought the house next door! That was huge. And had huge implications for him being around more. Her turn to blow out a breath.

How he spent his money could not affect

her. She wouldn't let it, or she could try not to let it. But holy heck.

And there was more. What was his third request? What more could he want? 'And the last?'

He paused. 'I would like Chloe to know I am her father before I leave to return to Italy. In fact, I would like her to know now, but...' Another shrug. 'I agree to wait until you decide the time is right, as long as it is before I leave.'

And there it was.

The endgame. She could understand that. And he obviously had real plans to return to see his daughter in the future—he'd started proceedings to become a property owner—she had no valid reason not to confirm his relationship to her daughter. But the thought sat, terrifying her like a black hole of unknown depth just the same.

What if he let Chloe down?

What if Chloe began to want something she couldn't have?

Even more terrifying. What if Faith did?

'I have no control over your second condition except it would have been more sensible to buy her an expensive doll's house, not a real one. Your third request I will consider and let you know tonight. I can understand you wanting her to know.'

'Thank you.' He stood. 'I have given you much to think about.'

Yes. He had given her a lot to think about. And did she want him to arrive with them as a part of their party at the barbecue later? No real choice. He was in their life. Now. Probably for ever.

He looked a little uncertain and, even in their short acquaintance, she could see it sat oddly on him. 'Do you still wish me to join you tonight, at your friend's dinner?'

'Of course.' She looked at him with a resigned expression. Shook her head. He was reading her mind again. 'I'll have to get used to you popping up out of the woodwork.'

'You will.' His eyes crinkled. 'And I will too. Pop up, as you say. Reappear with regularity. Regularity, that I promise.' His brows raised. 'I hope you grow to welcome my arrival.'

Welcome his arrival? Would she? A transference of awareness settled over her, as if from his aura to hers, a melding of their senses while not touching, as he captured her gaze with his. 'Let us see where this leads us, Faith. I will not let you down again.'

Her barriers quivered under the strain but held. 'As you say. We'll see.'

She watched his eyes narrow at her less than trusting response.

He held out his palm and reluctantly she took his strong fingers in hers and his warmth seeped into her like it had from the first moment they'd met years ago—until their hands separated, slowly.

She tucked her fingers behind her back. 'We'll leave here by six. It won't be a late night. Chloe gets tired.'

Instead of stepping away, he stepped closer, his bulk blocking out the light from the open door. His male scent coated with the salt of the sea. His strong jaw coming closer as he leaned in and she turned her head until he kissed her cheek. His breath was warm on her face, his mouth even warmer, and despite herself her body softened even with that light touch. His hand came up and caressed the other side of her cheek, cupping her face with more warmth and such tenderness that slowly she turned her head towards him. Towards his full, sensuous mouth, until their lips were a breath apart. Inhaling the life force between them as they hovered on the brink of the kiss they shouldn't have.

Yet it was she who leaned forward and offered her mouth, her first sign of trust, her first forgiveness.

But it was he who propelled them slowly but surely into a kiss that buckled her knees and sent her hands up between them to clutch his shirt. His arms came around her with a certainty and possession that jammed them together until her breasts were hard against his rock-like chest. She wanted to be lost like this so much.

She pushed him away.

He stilled at once. Nodded, turned and left before she could make her feet move. Her breath eased out. She sagged against the door she moved to shut.

Phew.

She glanced down at the table and a small package lay there.

Her brow furrowed as she opened the door again and called out to him softly, 'You left something.'

He turned and his smile lit his dark, handsome face and made her knees weaken again. 'It is a small gift for Chloe when she wakes.'

She held the package but almost forgot it in her hands as she watched him walk away. That kiss. They could have ended up in bed if she'd let that go on.

A kiss that had shattered her reserves. Thank goodness she'd managed to cling onto the extremely tattered remains of her protective coat by a few wispy threads. See. This was the problem with the man. Once he touched she became lost on the ocean of his expertise.

She hated that. She'd been like seafoam in his hands until the thought had crashed in that this had happened before. That he couldn't be trusted, despite her body telling her he could. But why did she lean into the kiss knowing this?

She should regret that kiss but in her heart she knew she didn't. And even more worrying was the fact she didn't care that she held no regrets.

She wrapped her arms around her middle and stared at the closed door as if it were the man who had just left. How did this change things for her, for Chloe, for them as a family?

If she didn't know the answer to that, then thank goodness she'd pushed him away.

CHAPTER ELEVEN

WHEN CHLOE WOKE an hour later she wandered out of her room, rubbing her pale face with small fists. Faith saw the moment she realised only her mother was there and their visitor had departed while she'd slept.

'Has Mr Salvanelli gone?'

The sudden droop to her daughter's mouth gave Faith a pang in her stomach.

'Yes, darling. But he'll be back tonight.' She suppressed a worried sigh. Already he was charming her daughter too.

'Oh. Okay. He's nice.' Chloe's gaze landed on the small parcel Raimondo had left. 'What's that?'

'Mr Salvanelli said it was for you. A present he thought you might like.'

'For me?' She hopped up and down and then hurried towards it, just as Izzy came in through the front door. 'Aunt Izzy, I have a present!'

Chloe caressed the tissue-wrapped gift carefully. 'Can I open it?' This to Faith.

'Yes. Open it.'

Faith's eyes met those of her aunt. 'Hello, Izzy. Raimondo left Chloe a present while she was sleeping.'

'Nice of him.' They both watched Chloe burrow through the tissue paper carefully. Luckily there was only one piece of tape so it didn't take too long.

While they waited Faith asked, 'How's Myra?'

'Good. Looking forward to tonight. I hear we're all going up to Reg's impromptu party.

'Raimondo is coming.'

Izzy's brows rose.

'Oh, she's beautiful!' Chloe's reverent voice interrupted them. She spun to show her mother and aunt the gaily dressed Italian peasant doll. 'Look at her apron. And her scarf and hat.' The red touches did make the little figure glow with colour.

'Lovely, darling,' Faith said and suppressed another exhalation. This was just the beginning.

'She must be from Italy.' Her aunt was

watching her. Faith avoided her aunt's eye and looked at her daughter. Forced a gay smile.

'She needs a name and she should meet all your other little dolls.'

Chloe nodded seriously. 'She doesn't have blonde hair but I'm going to call her Elsa. Like in *Frozen*.' Chloe clutched the doll to her chest.

'Elsa is a lovely name,' Faith said. 'Why don't you take her into your room and show her to your other dolls?'

Chloe flashed a brilliant smile at them both and dashed off.

Izzy tilted her head at Faith. 'You look like you need a cup of tea.'

'I think I need two.' She lowered her voice to a whisper. 'He's put a deposit on a house here. Next door.'

Izzy's startled eyes flew to Faith's from the hot water jug she'd been plugging in. 'The Captain's house? Right next door?' Saw the confirmation in Faith's face. 'Good grief!'

Faith nodded heavily. 'Apparently for Chloe. In trust.'

'Did you tell him a doll's house would have been more sensible?'

Faith felt the burden of her worry lighten. She had to laugh. She loved her aunt. 'I did, actually.'

'Well.' Izzy finished plugging in the appliance and came across to hold out her hands for Faith to take. Izzy's warm squeeze of her fingers settled her thumping heart. 'He seems a good man. You wouldn't have been attracted to him if he hadn't been. Perhaps just see where this leads? I guess this means he's planning on sticking around.' Izzy dropped her hands and patted her shoulder.

'I don't see that. He'll return to Italy, leaving us all unsettled again. Including Chloe now. I'm worried this means he's planning on popping in and out of our lives like a jack-in-the-box.'

They both looked towards Chloe's room, where the sound of animated one-sided conversation carried on. Quietly Izzy pointed out, 'She does need a father.'

'And he wants me to tell Chloe before he leaves.'

Izzy nodded. As Faith knew she would. 'I think that's fair. Now that we all know he's invested, literally, but also I believe emotionally in finding his daughter.'

Faith closed her eyes for a second to centre herself. To calm, and be sensible, like she normally was. But again that man had thrown her life into turmoil. She could see where Izzy's usual sense was leading. 'I believe he cares for her already too. And you're right. I know that. I just don't know how to tell her.'

Her aunt laughed. 'Darling. She's five. She'll take to the news as easily as she took to the doll. It's adults who complicate things.'

Izzy was probably right. In fact Faith knew she was. 'How did I get such a wise aunt?'

'Just lucky, I guess.' They hugged and stepped apart. 'Right. Tea.'

'Hold that thought. I should do it now.'

'May as well. Keep it simple.'

'Chloe?'

Chloe's head popped out of the room and then her whole body appeared. She had a doll in each hand. 'Susan and Elsa said they are going to be best friends.'

'That's lovely. Friends are very special. And I've got a secret to tell you.'

Chloe scooted right up to her mother. 'A secret?'

'Well, after I tell you it won't be a secret but it is true. Come sit with me.' She drew her daughter across to the settee and then onto her lap as they sat. She couldn't help a last glance at her aunt, who waved her on. Her heart thumped in her chest as she smoothed her daughter's hair. Inhaled the scent of her baby beside her.

'Do you remember me telling you that before you were born your daddy had to go away and wasn't ever able to come back here? That we wrote to him when you were born but he still couldn't come.'

Chloe's little brow furrowed and her big eyes blinked as she concentrated on her mother's serious tone. 'Yes.'

'Good.' A quick glance to Izzy and another deep breath. 'Well, he still lives away, but it seems that sometimes he *will* be able to visit us.' And she'd better add one of those big forced smiles here. She actually felt like crying as she watched her daughter process the information. Then the little face beside her jerked up as the penny dropped.

'My daddy? My real daddy? Like Piper has a daddy and Emily has a daddy?'

Oh, good grief, Faith thought, and her heart cracked. 'Yes. Though he won't be living with us like that. But you will be able to write to him. And maybe talk to him on the phone sometimes.'

'And he'll visit. And I'll be able to see him?'

'Sometimes.' Faith thought her heart would break for her little girl, who'd missed out on a daddy like Piper and Emily but liked the idea of a part-time parent zooming in and out of their lives because she knew no better. Izzy must have sensed that because she came and sat down beside them both.

Izzy said brightly, 'I think a daddy who can come sometimes is still better than a daddy who is never here. What do you think, Chloe?'

Chloe glanced at Izzy. 'Yes.' Though Faith thought her daughter didn't sound too sure.

Izzy waved Faith on. 'Simple,' she mouthed.

'Anyway. The secret is…' in a rush '… Mr Salvanelli is your father and he's very excited to finally meet you and know you are his daughter.' The words were out, never to be taken back, and Chloe stared at her.

'Really?' Her daughter frowned, searched her mother's face as if sensing Faith's mixed feelings.

'Yes. Really.'

'That's exciting. It must be why he gave me the doll.' Her hand slipped into her mother's and small fingers tightened around hers. Chloe's big green eyes searched Faith's face. 'But you're still going to be my mummy, aren't you?'

Faith hugged Chloe to her, the soft floating hair surrounded her, the tiny body wiggled in closer. 'Yes, my darling baby.' She smoothed Chloe's silken hair again, the strands so precious under her fingers. 'I will always be your mummy and I will always be here for you.'

Chloe slipped her arms around Faith and squeezed her back and then wriggled away. 'I'll have a daddy here for my birthday. That's lovely. Can I go play with my dolls again now?'

Faith's eyes met Izzy's and she blinked away the emotion that clouded her vision. Her daughter's world was secure. She wished her own world was as simple.

'Yes. Off you go.'

Two hours later, as he strode uphill towards Faith's house, Raimondo knew his life was about to change in ways he'd only ever imagined in weak moments. He was a father. A real family with warmth and joy and he was a part of it.

His axis had already shifted, meeting Faith again and being forcibly reminded by her beauty and calm how much they had connected so briefly so long ago. And earlier today.

That kiss.

Dios, that kiss.

He must not be distracted.

Because now, knowing of his daughter, he was already growing to love the child. She was such a beautiful young girl and he only hoped Chloe would come to love him when she knew him.

For his daughter was easy to love, like the mother had been almost six years ago, though he hadn't known at the time the indelible imprint Faith Fetherstone would have on his soul.

And on his life. On his future. He should have been here earlier.

His daughter. He crossed his fingers behind his back. Now he was being childish, but perhaps Faith had already told his daughter since he'd seen them this afternoon and Chloe would call him *papà*.

Though he couldn't help but wonder if he deserved such kindness.

He stopped outside the house with the sold sign. Barely saw the neglected gardens and peeling paint on the old weatherboards. *Pah*, it would fix with money. He glanced up at the turret that looked over the top of Faith's house and out to the sea. Remembered his daughter's words and the synchronicity of his purchase before he had even heard them.

A castle for his princess. He imagined his daughter looking though the polished brass telescope he would buy her, perhaps standing on a set of wheeled steps until she grew of a height, but excited and pointing at a passing ship. Yes. He could see that.

And that wasn't all he could see—though this part was more fanciful. He saw her beautiful mother watching fondly, imagined all the things in the wide world he could show them both. The Italy he could show them. The life they could share. If they'd let him. Patience. Already he was bursting with impatience.

It was still difficult to comprehend he had left Faith pregnant, that Maria had hidden the letters Faith sent; that his wife had kept such a secret from him was too petty to comprehend. Too cruel.

He could not imagine the hardships his child's mother, his Faith, had to endure, the judgements he'd exposed her to with his carelessness, but he would not sour this coming evening with bitter thoughts. His daughter waited.

He started walking again and his stride lengthened until he turned into the gate of Faith's house.

As he reached up to knock his fingers on the white wooden door, it opened. His miracle of a daughter stood there, her excited face tilted sideways, her dark hair pulled back and tied with a yellow ribbon, her tiny pink mouth pursed as she studied him. Then she smiled.

'What a pretty ribbon,' he said, more to see her smile widen than anything else.

'Yellow is my favourite colour.' Then, without pause, 'Thank you for my doll. Mummy said you're my daddy. Is that right?'

His heart jumped in his chest and he wanted to lift her and swing her up, hug her to his chest, but instead he was careful not to expect too much and said, '*Sì*. That is right. I am your *papà*, and I am very glad to have found you.'

'So? Can I tell my friend, Piper?'

'Of course. If your mother is fine with that.' He looked past his daughter to Faith as she hovered protectively, as any mother would when an almost-stranger wanted to claim half her child. She was incredible, this woman. Brave. Honest. His heart swelled.

'Thank you,' he said quietly, and she nodded and gestured him in.

'Excuse me,' Chloe's voice piped up. 'Do I have any brothers or sisters or cousins? Or grandparents? Piper has cousins and grandparents.'

'I'm afraid not, Chloe. You do have an Uncle Dominico in Italy. But he has no family.' He caught Faith's eye and shook his head slightly. He didn't want Chloe to become sad with the history of loss in his family.

'So my Uncle Dominico won't be here for my birthday?'

He smiled. 'No. I am sorry.'

An intense stare. 'But you will be?'

This he could say. 'Yes.'

She nodded once then looked back at him. 'Promise?'

His daughter's head was tilted and she looked suddenly like her mother. He moistened his lips to say yes, and then considered his first ever promise to his daughter. The magnitude of that. 'Unless the sky falls in.'

She nodded and he saw that she understood. Instead she said, 'Is my Uncle Dominico bigger than you?'

'No. We are the same size. But he is older. By ten minutes. He is my twin. Though sometimes he seems much older.'

Isabel stood against the window watching them, a small welcoming smile flashing briefly his way before she turned to give them privacy.

An odd fleeting thought crossed his mind. His brother would appreciate Isabel, if only he could get him here. How incongruous that this place across the world made him think of Dominico and his painful past.

'We're almost ready to leave.' Faith's voice brought him back to the present moment. 'It's just up the hill at the far croft.'

'I am ready. Today I will see one of the little houses on the edge of the cliffs—they intrigue me.'

She narrowed her eyes at him and said very softly, 'They are not for sale.' His purchase had obviously unsettled her. Then she went on, 'The views are spectacular, yes, and they're built from the same stone blocks as the lighthouse.'

He thought of the imposing structure on the far skyline across the bay. 'Your lighthouse is most picturesque.'

Faith smiled. Her tense posture eased a little and he was glad. 'I love it. The first time I saw it I felt like it stood benignly over a place I wanted to live. I came here for the work and found my world.'

He had thought that the first time he'd met her—how much she suited this little bay. Which was a problem in itself, but an issue for later. 'Then you are lucky. To feel at home is a special thing. As I walked here I was thinking that a telescope in the Captain's house would give a fine view as well.'

'I haven't been inside.' She turned to her aunt. 'Have you seen next door, Izzy?'

'Yes. Once.' Isabel gave him an assessing look. As if she too had thought his purchase too impulsive. 'Beneath the wear and tear there's lots of beautiful woodwork and the stairs are lovely. The view of the ocean from the turret is indeed impressive.'

Faith glanced at her watch. 'I'm sorry.

Time's marching on.' She picked up a small white-paper-wrapped parcel with a child's drawing covering it and shooed Chloe towards the door. 'Shall we go? We made some Rocky Road chocolate for Dr Southwell. He loves Rocky Road, doesn't he, Chloe?'

'He always has some in a jar.' His new daughter nodded enthusiastically and Raimondo had to smile. 'He says I make the best Rocky Road.'

She looked so pleased with herself and her mother smiled indulgently. He imagined the preparation of the sweets would be a shared task. 'I'm sure you do, little one.'

Raimondo's phone vibrated discreetly and he pulled the instrument from his pocket, frowning at the interruption. Dominico. He glanced at Faith. 'Excuse me, I must take this.' He turned to the doorway and stepped outside into the street.

'*Ciao*, Dominico.'

'Brother. Bad news. The factory has been destroyed. It lies in ruin.'

Raimondo sucked in a breath. His grandfather's legacy, which neither of them had wanted but both felt obliged to continue.

His brother answered the question before he could ask. 'Fire. I'm sorry. There are questions I cannot answer and I need you to return.'

No. He couldn't. Not yet. He glanced towards the family who were filing from the house towards him. He'd promised. 'This is difficult.' He lowered his voice. 'I gave my word to stay until Chloe's birthday tomorrow. It is only an extra twenty-four hours.'

Dominico's sigh sounded despairing. 'I'm sorry. The police wish to talk to us both.'

Pah. 'How can they expect me to travel so far for their whim? I will be back in two days.'

Another sigh. 'Then don't. It is just my need. This wearies me. Too much.'

Raimondo could hear the despair in his brother's voice. He was not the decisive and upbeat Dominico of old. He knew how hard it had been for his brother to climb back from his heartbreak, how he had buried his grief in becoming like his grandfather, lost in the business. Raimondo felt the tearing of himself in two as he wished to be in both places.

Was this the last straw? Dominico had worried him lately.

Yet he needed to stay for Chloe's birthday.

He needed to be there for his brother, who had always been there for him. He could feel his twin's pain across the distance between them. A hint of instability. A risk he could not take.

'If I come, will you travel with me to Australia when I return? A change of scenery may lighten your weariness and I have a young lady who wishes to meet her uncle.'

'I think not.'

'I think so. Or I will not come.'

'You must come.'

'Then we will discuss it soon. Arrange for a friend to stay with you until I arrive. You must promise this.'

'As you wish.' A weary agreement, not a happy one.

'Done. Have Rosa arrange the flights. I will leave in a few hours to make the midnight flight from Brisbane tonight, use Singapore.'

'Sì.' A pause. 'Thank you.'

'Look after yourself until I arrive. Yes?'

'Yes.'

'*Ciao.* Now to tell my daughter I must break my promise I have only just made.' He ended the call.

It was the mother who would be angry on her daughter's behalf, and he didn't blame her. He just hoped the rapport they had begun to enjoy would not be damaged, but he knew it would.

Knew he had done damage to the fledgling trust she had offered him today and he cursed fate and fires and the lack of free will.

CHAPTER TWELVE

FAITH LOOKED UP from straightening Chloe's hair to the man waiting at the gate. There was something in his face that said all was not well. Deep inside she knew she wasn't going to like this and her heart began to pound. 'Everything all right, I hope?'

He looked at her and the worry and frustration in his eyes forewarned her. Her stomach sank. 'A fire. The company headquarters have been destroyed in Florence. My brother asks that I return immediately.'

And so it begins.

Of course he would go. She'd known that. 'When?'

'Tonight. Later.' Faith sucked in her breath as he finished with, 'I will fly at midnight.'

Hot words wanted to pour out but she wouldn't let them. She'd expected this, hadn't she? She looked at her daughter, who had skipped ahead with Izzy. Instead of berating him, she said calmly, 'Before Chloe's birthday?'

'*Sì*. My apologies.'

'I expected nothing from you.' Her tone said she was unsurprised. She raised her brows and as her heart iced over she shot him a cold look. 'And it is not me you need to apologise to. Perhaps you'd better tell her before she tells all and sundry you'll be at her party.'

Raimondo winced and glanced at his daughter, a few large strides ahead, chatting to her aunt.

Faith seethed. As well he should consider Chloe. Broken promise number one. That hadn't taken long. She felt like stamping her foot and asking if one more day would make such a difference. But of course he would go.

'Chloe?' Faith called and Chloe skipped back down to them. 'Your father has something to tell you. You walk with him here and I'll talk to Aunty Izzy about something she needs to know.' Because if she didn't move away she was going to say something she regretted and Chloe was the important one. She was the one who had told him that.

She turned and walked a little too quickly back to where Izzy was admiring a rose bush in the next-door garden but Raimondo and Chloe's voices carried on the still air. She'd known his priorities so why was she surprised?

'He has to leave for a family emergency.' She could hear the tartness and was glad she'd spoken softly to Izzy. They both turned to see how Chloe took it.

She heard him say, 'Chloe, I am so sorry that I must break my first promise to you. Something has happened in my home town and I have to leave and go back to Italy before your birthday.'

Chloe's face fell and then she furrowed her brows. 'You said you would be here. Did the sky fall in? Like *Chicken Little*?'

He stopped and crouched down to her level. '*Sì*, little one. You are very clever. The sky has fallen in on our factory because of a bad fire and I must help my brother sort the mess.'

Chloe's face creased. 'In the story the sky didn't really fall.' Faith heard the forlorn note in her daughter's words and her eyes narrowed at Raimondo. She hoped she'd done the right thing agreeing to his request of access but she didn't see how she could have done any different.

Raimondo nodded solemnly. 'But in Italy this has really happened. Though when I have finished the sorting I will return as fast as I can. And perhaps bring your Uncle Dominico as well. But I am very sad that I cannot be here for your birthday tomorrow, little one. I broke a promise, which is not good.'

Chloe sighed and shrugged her shoulders with resignation. 'It's not broken if the sky fell in.'

Faith felt tears prickle behind her eyes as her young daughter behaved so very kindly. Watched Chloe tuck her hand in his. 'But you are coming tonight to the party and I can tell Piper you are my daddy. And you said you will be back.'

Faith heard it all. Tried to be as philosophical as her five-year-old daughter and struggled.

Izzy squeezed her hand and made her walk forward up the hill. 'Come on. Let's go ahead or we'll be late.'

The party was in full swing when they arrived. Reg and Myra met them at the door, and it seemed half of the Lighthouse Bay hospital was in attendance inside. The other half must be working, Faith thought with a forced smile at another of her colleagues.

She couldn't help notice the curious glances Raimondo drew. A stranger and a darkly attractive one at that. Plus he'd actually been present for a birth and two resuscitations as well. He'd been busy in the short time he'd been here. He'd been busy with her too, and even more she regretted that kiss. She sighed.

Of course the first thing Chloe did was drag Piper across to Raimondo and announce in a loud voice, 'He's my real dad. He's from Italy so I call him *Papà*, not Daddy. He has to go home tonight but he's coming back soon.'

And that pretty well sums it up, Faith thought as she felt the heat push past her chest, up her neck and into her cheeks. Piper's mouth fell open, along with the half a dozen people in earshot.

Izzy laughed.

Trina, Faith's friend and fellow midwife, and Piper's stepmother, held her pregnant belly and laughed as well. Then she sent a quizzical look Faith's way. 'Gotta love kids.'

She put out her hand and Raimondo took her fingers and shook. 'So, you're Chloe's dad, not just a friend. That explains a lot.'

'It does?'

'It will,' she said cryptically and Faith knew she was in for a grilling. 'Welcome, Raimondo, even though we already met at the beach this morning,' Trina said with a laugh. 'I'm sure Faith will fill us in on the details.' Then she clapped her hands. 'Everyone! Please meet Raimondo Salvanelli, a GP from Florence and a friend of the Fetherstones.'

She turned to the tall man who had come up at the commotion. 'Finn, darling. It seems Raimondo is Chloe's surprise daddy, all the way from Italy.'

Finn glanced at Faith of the red cheeks. Then he met Raimondo's eyes and nodded. 'Kids. I'm the local paediatrician so I understand them a little. I see your daughter has taken my daughter's hand after causing a stir and blithely run off to play dolls.'

'As children do,' Raimondo said with a smiling glance in his Chloe's direction. Then he looked towards her. 'Her mother is equally charming.'

Faith rolled her eyes. Not that easy,

buddy, she thought, and was touched when Finn championed her.

'Faith is well appreciated here.' There was no force in the statement but Raimondo nodded at the gentle warning.

'Unfortunately, I must leave tonight, but I will return soon to better acquaint myself with Chloe and renew my acquaintance with Faith.'

Good lord, that almost sounded like a statement of claim and Faith resisted the urge to call him on it. She was the calm one. She was the one in control here. He was the blow-in.

'We look forward to knowing you better.' Finn shook his hand. 'Another doctor in town is always good. And my dad said you did well. We don't have emergencies often here but handy to know when there's extra help in the bay.'

'I'll make sure I'm accredited with your government for such times. The Electronic Portfolio of International Credentials have my CV for the aid work I do, so it should be possible.'

'Excellent. Come, and I'll introduce you.'

Raimondo followed Finn and Faith sagged a little now all announcements of Chloe's paternity were out of her hands. There was no going back from here.

'You've had a wild couple of days. And then he leaves?' Trina linked her arm. 'Come on, I'll get you a nice glass of Sav Blanc even though I can't join you. Ellie said Raimondo popped up at one of your cave tours. Must have been a shock.'

Faith looked at her friend. Saw no judgement, just sympathy. 'Understatement. Apparently, the letters I sent didn't make it to him. It was Sam's sister's Italian guests from your wedding who started the chain reaction. I could say this is all your fault.'

Trina held up her hands and laughed. 'Francesca? My bad. But he is a bit of a dish. I can see how he must have been tempting if he turned all that charm on you. What were you? Twenty?'

'First year out of uni.' Faith took the crystal glass Trina handed her with a nod of thanks. 'He has charm. But the gloves are off if he disappoints Chloe.'

'I'm sure he knows that. Though Chloe is tough like her mother. And her aunt. You've laid good groundwork there for your daughter's coping ability.'

Faith looked at her friend and felt a swell

of emotion. For the last twenty-four hours her feelings had been like the waves outside the window. Rolling in one after another. No wonder she was feeling buffeted by Raimondo's arrival. But Trina's belief in her daughter felt reassuring. And similar to Izzy's confidence. 'Thank you. I hope so.'

'Let him do all the work, Faith. You've done your bit. Just enjoy the ride.'

She almost choked. 'The ride? Good lord. I feel like I'm learning to surf and a big wave is going to knock me off the board and pummel me to bits.'

'Not you. You have great balance. Besides, you have plenty of friends to help keep you afloat.'

'Okay. Let's go see what new challenge has appeared with Raimondo loose in the room and my daughter telling all and sundry.'

'You've got this. There's only friends here,' Trina replied as she linked arms again.

Raimondo shook hands and responded to the kindness as he was introduced to many and moved through the room and out into the sunny backyard where tables and chairs were scattered. He had a beer in his hand bestowed by Finn, children played on a swing set in the corner and the ocean stretched away like a tufted blue carpet.

This was so different to the formality of his world in Florence.

The salt air made him breathe deeply, as did the sight of Faith coming towards him with Finn's wife. He knew now he could have done this better with some warning to her and certainly it would have been better not to rush away tonight. He stamped down the frustration his impending journey caused. The sooner he left, the sooner he could come back.

He watched her approach, this woman from the past whom he wanted in his future. So beautiful, and he could see she tried hard to be light and calm when he had certainly complicated her serene world.

'Here you are,' she said quietly. 'How have you survived the gauntlet of Lighthouse Bay medical community?'

'I have been made most welcome.'

Someone called out to Finn and Trina. Trina said, 'See you soon,' and the couple waved and moved away.

Raimondo kept his eyes on Faith. 'Thank you for allowing me to meet your friends.'

Faith spread her hands. 'There was a gathering. We do it a lot and you were here.'

'I have made this very confronting for you, have I not?'

'Yes.' She half laughed when she really wanted to cry. 'Our past relationship is certainly out there for public consumption. But Chloe did need to know her dad existed so I guess I had hoped this would happen at some time.'

'I am truly sorry I leave tonight.'

Her green eyes studied him as if to seek the truth of his words. But she didn't say anything. What could she say?

He was a fool to leave but he would ensure it didn't happen again. The more he saw her, the more he needed to know more. He needed to be with her longer to understand the woman Faith had become and rearrange his priorities. But he'd needed to reassure Dominico that he would be there soon. A frisson of fear reminded him he could not delay this trip—he needed to see his brother for himself. And ensure something had been put in place that would keep Dominico safe until he arrived.

Chloe appeared beside them and snuggled into her mother and yawned. Softly, Faith patted her head. 'You're tired, sweetheart.'

Raimondo shot a glance at his new daughter. Saw her paleness. She had already slept today. 'Always tired?'

Why tired?

Faith met his questioning look. 'Chloe had a nasty cold two weeks ago and she's been easily worn out since then. She's taking vitamins and getting sunshine, and she's been good about resting.'

He heard the tiny thread of worry under the light description of illness. Felt his own concern stir. Grow suddenly huge. Had a sudden memory of his brother's devastation at the loss of his son. No. This would not happen when he had just found them. 'Has she had blood tests for this?'

Faith looked down at her daughter. 'Yesterday morning before preschool. We have an appointment with Uncle Finn on Monday for the results, don't we, Chloe, before I go to work.'

Chloe nodded and yawned again. Faith turned the child away from him towards the door. He said very quietly, 'This is the first you tell me of this?'

Faith raised her brows at him. 'Yes. Thank you for your concern. Chloe and I will say our goodbyes inside. You don't need to come with us. Have a comfortable flight tonight.'

He bit back an instinctive command it would have been very foolish to issue. Yes, he'd erred in that question, been undiplomatic, but he felt the slap of not having rights and knew it was his own fault. 'I will come with you now.'

Faith paused and turned back to him. 'And if I don't want you to?'

He shrugged. 'I will follow anyway.'

So he shadowed them and nodded his goodbyes along with Faith and Chloe. Isabel, Raimondo noted, was observant of his presence beside them and chose to leave them to continue their departure unaccompanied.

No doubt she would have left with her niece if Faith had been alone.

He truly appreciated her understanding.

While Raimondo waited in the open lounge Faith had ushered Chloe straight to bed.

As he paced the room for her to come back he considered all that had happened over the last two days, the enormous change to his life and his future plans. That shock of seeing Faith again and her effect on him, the way the world had suddenly opened up in the most marvellous and unexpected way with the confirmation of his being a father.

But now the bombshell of Chloe's strange lethargy. All this and he was leaving!

He needed to plan his return, assess his options for gaining further information on his daughter while he was away. Especially as he'd almost alienated Faith with his stupid accusation of her withholding Chloe's illness from him.

So how to approach this new turn sensibly?

He stared at the photo album lying on the table. The urgency of responsibilities he wanted to share ate at him.

Firstly, Faith needed to be able to contact him in any emergency. *Dios*, imagine if something happened to Chloe, something he could help with, and she couldn't access him. It didn't bear thinking about.

Twitching with suppressed urgency, he pulled a business card and a small pen from his wallet and crossed to the table to lean on the surface.

Faith needed his personal mobile number, though that would help little on the flight. Then he wrote his home number as well on the back of the card. The business number was on the front and Dominico would have set up a temporary phone office at least. He thought again and wrote Dominico's details down as well.

Now the numbers he needed. He produced a new card and wrote Faith, Isabel, Finn. He needed the paediatrician's last name as a contact. By the time he'd made his list Faith had returned.

'She's asleep.'

What if his daughter was truly unwell? A surge of panic, a premonition swamped him suddenly, perhaps because he'd seen so much loss and this could not go that way. Unease twisted in his stomach and made his tone more forceful than it should have been. 'Asleep already?'

Faith's brows went up at his doubting tone. 'As I said. I'm not lying.'

He pulled himself back. 'This is not what I mean. I do not doubt you. But her lethargy. What are your thoughts?'

He watched the lowering of her stiff shoulders as she passed a hand across her brow and sighed and now another emotion swamped him. This was not easy and everything had happened very fast for her—he'd had time to consider the impending reconnection.

Suddenly he wanted to take her in his arms and console her. Tell her all would be well, as any father would console a mother, but he didn't have that right. And they didn't know that.

'Faith, I'm sorry.' He stepped closer. 'For everything.' He put one hand on her arm. 'You have done everything right and I'm not saying this well.'

She interrupted him. 'I'm sure she's fine.' She said what they both prayed. 'We will have the results on Monday and make sure.'

Yes. Monday. Two days' time. When he would be over the ocean and thousands of miles away—though he could email from the aircraft if needed. Even telephone if the conditions were right.

'How will I get the results?' He needed Finn's number. He reached across and placed the business card in her hand. 'These contact details allow you to find me any time.' He handed her the other card.

'Please may I have yours and Finn's numbers? And perhaps Isabel if I cannot contact you?' Had that come out too abruptly?

She looked at him. Cocked her head at his insistent tone. 'I will give you the house telephone number, and my mobile,' she said slowly. 'But I would prefer to share Chloe's results with you myself rather than have you contact Finn.'

More delay. 'That is not acceptable to me.'

Her hand brushed her face again. 'Let me think.'

He lifted his chin. 'Fine. There is no need. I will find out for myself. It is no secret where we are and who the paediatrician in this town is.' He regretted the words as soon as they left his lips.

She narrowed her eyes at him. 'So. Is this the real Raimondo Salvanelli? Are you trying to intimidate me? In my own home?'

'That is not my intention.' Impatience was still in his tone and he tried to rein it back. He could not lose Chloe now.

'Isn't it? Then why are you ordering me

around? Laying down laws? You have no say over me.'

He lifted his chin at her. 'My daughter may be unwell and I will not be told at your convenience.'

Her eyes widened. 'Chloe is my daughter and I will let you know the result of the test when I get it.' Her voice held warning and again he saw she was not the diffident girl he'd met nearly six years ago.

'Though—' here a flash of unusual anger in her eyes '—of course you can go behind my back and source them from Finn.'

'Stop.' He held up his hand. How had it come to this? His fault. Doing this wrong. 'You are right.' He ran his hands through his hair, almost pulling it free from its roots. 'My fault. We are friends. Were once more. Your kindness has astounded me and I repay you with this impatience. My apologies.' He touched her arm. 'Forgive me.'

When she looked at him he could see the shimmer of distress, and possibly fear for her daughter, in her eyes and it pierced him with an arrow of protective instinct that surged from his very soul.

Of course she was terrified that Chloe was unwell.

Of course he wasn't helping by being demanding.

Unable to stop himself, he reached out and very slowly, very surely, he drew her against his chest into what he hoped was a comforting embrace. He needed to reassure her he cared.

'I want to be here for you and Chloe.'

'What if when you leave you become caught up in your other life again?' Her voice was so uncertain it stabbed him. 'What if I have to tell Chloe you've forgotten her, like you forgot me?'

It stabbed him again. 'I never forgot you. You have always been a part of a shining star which went home with me nearly six years ago and I tucked that star into my heart and never forgot you.'

She shook her head against him. 'I find that hard to believe.' Her voice was very soft.

'I'm not surprised.' He stroked her hair. 'But it is true.'

His fingers continued to stroke her silky head as she laid her cheek against him, not pulling back as he'd feared she would, and he remembered the feel of her against him from so long ago. The kiss of earlier. The feel of her skin under his fingers triggering memories and transporting him. Her scent was so sweet, her smooth flesh so right in his arms. Perfect.

Too perfect not to act on. His grip tightened with one arm and with the other hand, so slowly, he tilted her chin upwards.

'What if I said when I come back I will never leave you and our daughter again?'

Now he could look down into her face. He waited for her answer as he lost himself in the green pools of her siren's eyes. Could not resist the stretch of his thumb to so gently trace the soft, trembling curve of her pink lips. So beautiful.

'No answer?'

A shake of her head. 'How can I believe that?'

'When I come back I will convince you. For now I must do this task for my brother and tie up some ends that need to be complete. For the moment, begin to trust. At least try.'

'I'll try.'

As her body softened against his he too loosened the bands of the restraint that had been crushing him and lowered his head. Their breath mingled and their mouths touched and finally, after so long being lost, he found the one place for him that was home.

CHAPTER THIRTEEN

RAIMONDO'S MOUTH AGAINST hers felt like a homecoming. Her arms wrapped around him. How had she spent so long without this in her life? How had she spent so long without this man in her life?

That scent of Raimondo against her, something she remembered from the last time they'd kissed, the warmth of his whisper on her cheek as he brushed her face with light kisses before returning to her mouth. The heat in his lips as he gently nudged his tongue against hers and she opened her mouth to him.

Her knees wobbled as he drew her into him and all Faith could do was close her eyes and hang on.

It was just a kiss. Again.

And another kiss. So, with each gentle probe or tender stroke, she forgot more of the world outside his embrace. Took comfort from the craziness of the last few days of turmoil in the last place she'd expected to find shelter from the fear in her heart.

Her hands left his waist to splay against his solid upper body and then curled into his shirt, straining him closer. Her breasts pushed almost painfully into his chest and through their clothes the heat between their skin built into a slow cauldron of need that swirled in on itself, creating a whirlpool of desire drawing her deeper. It had been so long since she'd felt a strong man's arms about her. So long since Raimondo had taught her the secrets of this place. Too long if she responded like this.

From just a kiss.

Faith dragged her mouth reluctantly from his and searched his face. His beautiful eyes. Saw the aroused darkness of desire and promise to transport them both to a place she'd almost forgotten existed. A wisp of fear curled around her. She wasn't sure she could survive from revisiting the magic if he walked away afterwards and never came back.

'Should we do this?'

'Should we not?' His voice as bemused as hers.

'What is this between us?'

'Destiny. Tonight I will be gone, but I will be back.'

A cold tendril of foreboding touched her with a chill.

Abruptly it hit her that accidents happened, aeroplanes crashed, moments were to be grasped. Fleeting opportunities to be loved by someone were like clouds that you reached for in the sky and suddenly she didn't want this ray of hope for the future to pass without grasping the possibilities. If something happened to Raimondo now, how would she survive if she knew she could have had this?

'Make love to me before you go.'

Raimondo's eyes darkened even more and bored into hers. 'My most burning desire.'

'Please.' The word floated from her mouth in a whisper, barely heard, barely believable, and yet brazenly sure. She needed to feel his arms around her one more time before he left because inside she still wasn't sure Raimondo would ever be back and, regardless of the pain to come, she wanted this from him.

The ground disappeared from beneath her feet as he swept her up, carried her tenderly, and she rested her cheek against his chest, listening to the strong beat of his heart to drown out the voices clamouring in her head.

With infinite care he lowered her to the bed and joined her.

CHAPTER FOURTEEN

ON SUNDAY MORNING, twelve hours after he'd left, Faith lay on the same crumpled bed where she had made love with Raimondo and stared at the fluffy clouds passing in the small gap in the curtains, not seeing them. What she saw was a glorious, tumultuous storm of reconnection, the gentle whispers, the tender caresses—all the reasons they had both been crazy before—the memories now returned to heat her cheeks and make her draw her arms to cradle her stomach as she mourned the loss of Raimondo beside her.

Put simply, wrapped together they made magic.

So she couldn't regret the pure joy of it or the risk to her heart in the making. But where would it end? She had given herself to him before he'd left, their mutual need overcoming their reserve, perhaps each seeking the reassurance holding the other would give. But it had been more. It had been everything they'd found before, with greater poignancy because of the past mistakes he'd made. Their combined worry for Chloe, the risk to the family that was so close to being possible. She saw that it had been hard for him to tear himself away, hard for him to look one last brief time at his sleeping daughter, and she didn't doubt that it would be hard to drive from Lighthouse Bay and catch a plane.

It had been a few days of craziness again.

The upheaval to her life that ridiculously gorgeous Italian man could create in forty-eight action-packed hours. He'd better come back. At least she was sure she was covered for contraception this time.

But he would be back. He'd promised. Chloe would have a dad. And Faith? What would she have?

She shifted to sit up. *That way madness lies...* She couldn't imagine yet.

Now, it was the morning of Chloe's birthday and the sun crept fingers of soft yellow up the wall of her bedroom so she should rise and try to ease the new memories Raimondo had created back into her secret place for later. It was going to be a beautiful November day for a children's party.

How fast those five years had flown since her baby had been born—and hadn't their lives been blessed with the joy of Chloe.

She wondered what the next five years would bring. Which drew her thoughts back to Raimondo.

To their kiss. And the progression from there.

Of course he stayed on her mind.

He would still be over the ocean on his flight, barely halfway to Italy, soon to land in Singapore. So no call had come yet for Chloe on her birthday. She would not think he had already relegated them to the back of his businessman's brain as the drama in Italy came closer. And was it so bad if he did; he'd said he needed to tie ends, sort out his many commitments before he could come back. He'd said he would be back—it was a shame a part of her didn't believe him. But that was for later.

She didn't care if he came back without his possessions. Wealth and assets did not have the same importance in her own life.

Though, she supposed, now she would

have to be more vigilant for Chloe to appreciate both sides of the financial coin if her father persisted in spoiling her with extravagant gifts.

Her daughter would not be spoiled by a rich man's whims. A little voice whispered that perhaps she was being harsh. She didn't want to listen. She'd been so darned unsettled since he'd arrived and even more unsettled since he'd left. Not surprising. Making love with Raimondo before he'd left had been an incredibly stupid, and incredibly wonderful, thing to do. It wasn't fair.

Chloe would wake soon, though, the way she had been sleeping in lately, one never knew.

Surely the lure of the enormous parcel that had arrived yesterday—on a Saturday; who knew how he had arranged that before he'd even known he would fly out?—would have her daughter up early. Obviously from Raimondo, and goodness knew what it would be in all its largeness and expensive express courier, but Chloe had been remarkably patient to wait until today to open it.

Like Christmas, she'd said.

Her little friends were arriving this morning at ten a.m. Faith had decided an early party would be more fun for Chloe than waiting around for the afternoon when she could be weary.

Dear Myra, a pastry chef and cake decorator in a past life before Lighthouse Bay, had made the 'Elsa from *Frozen*' cake and would bring the no doubt magnificent creation down at ten. Because it was Sunday, the adults would come for brunch after the children had been here an hour and done their party games, then they were having a sausage sizzle in the backyard which Finn had offered to cook for young and old.

It would be a typical extended family and friends day, held to celebrate one of theirs. All those coming who genuinely cared...

Raimondo should have been here to see his daughter's pleasure in being the star for the day.

But he wasn't. She shouldn't be surprised.

She shouldn't be disappointed.

Not at all. Really. But she was and not only for Chloe.

Faith pushed away the recently familiar flustered feeling in her stomach and opened the blinds properly to see the day.

Just as she thought. Glorious. She pushed open the window and the salt-laden air wafted into the room, forcing her to appreciate the good things. Forcing her to smile.

She loved living here. This was her home. Regardless of the ups and downs of the last few days, she was so very fortunate. And here came the footsteps of her precious daughter.

'Mummy, Mummy! It's my birthday!' A pink-pyjamaed missile fired through Faith's bedroom door and into her arms.

Faith hugged the warm tousled body into her and inhaled the tear-free shampoo scent of Chloe's soft hair. Her baby. Her life. 'Good morning, darling Birthday Girl. How exciting. Today you are how old…?' Faith pretended to scratch her chin.

'I'm five! I'm five!' Chloe bounced back off the bed and onto the balls of her feet and grinned at her mother. 'You're tricking.'

'Five? My goodness. So big. Off to school next year. But first—we have a party!'

Chloe's eyes rounded. 'I know! My first party. Piper said she has a present for me.'

'Well, that's very nice. You must remember to thank all the people for coming and also for presents and cards.'

'I will.'

Such a solemn vow, Faith thought with

amusement and stroked her daughter's soft cheek. Then she frowned at the small bruise on Chloe's neck.

'Did you bump yourself here?'

'Maybe.' Chloe was peering towards the kitchen and Faith let it go, though unease slid under her skin. 'Let's go and have breakfast and maybe you could open a present from me too. And one from Aunty Izzy.'

'And one from Mr Salvanelli. I mean *Papà*.' The little girl crinkled her forehead. '*Papà* is a funny word.'

'Maybe we can find a different word that works as well. But let's go see what we can find for your birthday breakfast.'

By eleven o'clock, when the adults were due to arrive, the presents had all been unwrapped and the children had begun to settle from the frenzy of pass the parcel. Everyone had a prize and the mood had calmed to staring with admiration at Chloe's wonderful cake and her wonderful doll's house.

Gift-wise, it seemed that Elsa and the *Frozen* story had won the day as well, with a set of *Frozen* dolls, a set of bed sheets, a *Frozen* duvet cover and even a cushion with Elsa's blonde head gazing out from it. It culminated with Raimondo's outrageously expensive *Frozen* castle doll's house, which impressed all the little girls mightily.

Faith remembered she'd suggested a doll's house, more fool her.

She thought of the three-storey, furnished, fantastical fairy tale extravaganza, and wondered how on earth he'd managed to order that and have it delivered in the space of a Saturday afternoon. It had proved well over-the-top but Chloe, of course, was ecstatic. Faith decided she'd need to talk to him about restraint with gifts—and she hadn't told her friends who had bought the Captain's house next door.

Soon enough when Raimondo took ownership, because then everyone would know.

She sighed. The man was turning into a headache of mammoth proportions. And heart-hugging secrets.

Trina and Finn were the parents who arrived last and Piper squealed and ran towards them with Chloe following. Until she slowed.

As if in slow motion, Chloe faltered, stopped and then silently she toppled sideways in a dead faint onto a discarded Elsa cushion, and Faith's heart missed a beat.

Faith reached out but she missed and by the time she knelt beside her daughter Finn was there too, easing her back. Faith didn't understand as her heart seemed to slowly gather momentum in her chest. What had happened?

His voice reached her shocked brain. Calm. Soothing. Like at work when that voice was directed at a patient, not at her. 'She's breathing, Faith. Fainted. Could just be excitement. I'll take her,' he said gently, 'to her bed. We'll look at her there.'

Then he lifted Chloe into his arms and carried Faith's baby away and she couldn't see her daughter's face as she hurried behind.

Once in the bedroom with the door closed, Finn examined Chloe and they found more bruises like the one Faith had seen that morning. Two on her belly and a dozen on her back and both lymph glands under her thin arms were suspiciously swollen.

When Chloe stirred from the faint, only a minute after she'd been put on her bed, she woke slowly, still groggy and vague.

Sadly, there would be no more birthday celebrations for Chloe.

Faith could hear Izzy in the distance as she ushered the guests out with a gentle, 'No, Chloe will be fine,' quietly dispersing the party behind the door as she took control. Her 'Thank you for coming' seemed surreal in the distance to Faith as she watched Finn examine Chloe with growing alarm that she tried to hide. Her anxiety ramped up to real terror as Finn took out his mobile phone and arranged emergency admission to the regional hospital for tests, but she smiled at Chloe and said, 'Uncle Finn knows best.'

But she was thinking, *My daughter is too sick for Lighthouse Bay Hospital.*

The ambulance ride took them to the base hospital and more blood tests were conducted.

Test results that proved serious enough to transfer her from the country to the city, and thankfully Faith was allowed in the aircraft too. So they both travelled by the rescue helicopter down to the Children's Hospital in Sydney.

As soon as they arrived, around three

p.m., Faith slipped outside the hospital to leave another message for Raimondo, this time at his place of work, and she jammed her phone up against her ear to try to block the noise of the traffic. She drew a deep breath as finally the long-distance call connected, and a woman's rolling accent answered at the other end.

'Salvanelli Compagnia Farmaceutica.'

Faith prayed the receptionist at his brother's temporary office could speak English. She had no Italian. 'I wish to speak to Dominico Salvanelli, please.'

'Signor Salvanelli is not available. I do not know when he will be back. I am sorry.' The accent was thick but the English perfect. Not that it helped.

That was it then. Raimondo's mobile phone and home number had only accepted voice messages as he would still be flying. She enunciated as clearly as she could, 'This is Faith Fetherstone from Australia. Please try to pass on a message to Dominico to contact his brother. Raimondo must phone me back as soon as possible. It is very urgent.'

So she'd done what she could about informing Raimondo and the forlorn hope that he would immediately begin his return to support her and Chloe through this terrifying ordeal had failed, as she should have expected. She would be alone.

No. That wasn't fair. Isabel would drive down as soon as she'd shaken her slight cold and the unacceptable risk of her infecting Chloe now she was so very susceptible.

Hours later, as visiting hours closed, the sounds of the Children's Hospital in Sydney made resting difficult on the chair beside Chloe's bed. Crying babies, toys being tossed or banged on the side of cots, the beeping of high-tech medical machines that whirred and trilled and the constant swish of nurses checking on her daughter.

At least no more fruitless time had been wasted on unsuccessful phone calls because now her phone was dead without her charger. She would concentrate on her daughter, as she should have been the last few days instead of being sidetracked by a man from her past.

Nine torrid hours after Chloe's collapse, on the longest day of Faith's life, Faith felt like a zombie as she paced the room. It was true that finally, after the terrifying provisional diagnosis, when acute myeloid leukaemia had been suggested at the regional hospital, and Faith had felt as if her body had turned to a lump of ice, things were tentatively looking up. Frozen-faced, she'd nodded, outwardly calm, and clutched Chloe's hand and they had to wait for more test results.

Now, after the bone marrow biopsy in Sydney, some hope for a different diagnosis seemed possible.

An hour ago Finn had phoned Faith on the ward phone with the results.

'The news is better than expected, Faith.'

She'd sagged against the wall, the ward phone clamped to her ear.

Finn went on. 'The latest tests and overall diagnostic pictures have pointed more towards a severe secondary bacterial infection on top of the recent viral infection. That combination mimicked the leukaemia symptoms.'

'Oh, my.' Faith had sagged further down the wall.

She'd almost missed the rest of Finn's news. 'The repeat blood tests still show Chloe's red cells are down and her white cells sky-high. That's why she's spiked that raging temperature.'

'The paediatrician here knows that?' She was trying to understand what this meant for Chloe.

'He rang me. He's been called to the operating theatre until later tonight. Sorry he couldn't tell you himself. We're cautiously hopeful that with the antibiotics Chloe will make a full recovery.'

Faith swallowed again the lump that had seemed lodged in her throat for hours. She hadn't been able to answer Izzy's questions when other calls had been brought to her, her mouth unable to form words as her throat closed. So Trina and Izzy had left messages.

'You need to rest, Faith. Try to sleep so you have reserves for tomorrow.'

She'd nodded and then realised he couldn't see her. 'Yes. I'll try.'

'What of Raimondo?'

'I left messages. He's still flying. Won't land until one a.m. tonight.'

'Hang in there. He'll be back.'

'It will take another two days at least. Thank you for ringing, Finn.'

'Get some rest.'

'Yes.' Then she'd hung up.

Raimondo would be very close to Florence, but that wouldn't help her. He was twenty-six hours' flight in the wrong direction.

But he could have rung the hospital at one of the stops. Despite the fact there was no wife to hijack her messages, he still hadn't answered.

She shouldn't be surprised he was not there for her.

Out of sight, out of mind.

She should have expected that.

The deep disappointment of Raimondo's absence sat in her chest like a stone. Didn't he know she needed strong arms and a chest to cry on at this moment as she watched their daughter sleeping with horror of her childish mortality so fresh in her mind?

Had that two days of upheaval he'd caused in her and Chloe's life meant nothing to him?

Faith stared at her daughter, weary tears she didn't have the energy to wipe as they dripped damply down her cheeks. Chloe's small fingers were tucked under her so pale chin and the other arm lay by her side strapped to the IV line with a bandage and a board to keep her arm straight. Her daughter shone ethereally white against the pillows, and all her mother could do was sit alone, watching, powerless to help her.

Two separate antibiotics were running through the drip she was connected to now the blood transfusion she'd needed was finished.

Still, the news was so much better than it could have been and now that she had allowed the hope to filter in, after the horrific dread that had filled her before, not unexpectedly, exhaustion swamped Faith. She put her head in her hands and closed her eyes.

They would beat this.

She and Chloe. They had to.

The door opened. It would be another nurse to check Chloe and she couldn't summon the energy to open her eyes.

'Faith.' A voice she knew.

Raimondo, looking slightly harried and slightly crumpled, very unlike himself, stood there, his hair mussed, his beautiful warm, reassuring eyes searching hers as he crossed the room towards her, his long strides eating up the distance between them.

Faith struggled to her feet. 'You're here?' Then she sagged and he crossed the last gap to catch her in his warm embrace.

CHAPTER FIFTEEN

RAIMONDO CROSSED THE room in a rush and pulled her into his arms and she sobbed against him. His strong hands held her as he pulled her against the chest she'd needed so much. Hugged her tighter to him until almost she couldn't breathe but it was so worth it as she felt the warmth of his body warming the chill that had soaked all the way into her bones.

His voice rumbled in her hair. 'I should never have left. I will not leave again unless I take you both with me.'

Faith didn't have the headspace to compute that. Her brain had shut down. She could only deal with this moment. 'She's been so sick.' Her voice sounded thick with tears, and relief, and exhaustion, but it felt so overwhelming that he'd come back. She'd hoped for a call and wasn't sure how he could have arrived but this was so much better than she'd hoped for.

'My poor Faith. The things I do to you without the intention to hurt you. I should never have left.'

'No, I wish you hadn't.' She looked up into his face. 'How are you back so quickly?'

He ran his hand through his hair at the memory. 'I flew back from Singapore. Your message appeared as we taxied in. I sent a doctor friend to sit with Dominico. That is another story. There was some dilemma as I retrieved my bags but it was arranged that instead of flying on I could change planes and fly back.'

'You must be exhausted.' The shadows under his eyes attested to that.

'Not like you. Not like Chloe. I should never have left,' he said again. They turned to stare at their daughter and his mouth compressed as he held back his emotion.

Faith touched his arm. 'You're here now.'

They crossed to the bed and Raimondo sat carefully on the edge and stroked Chloe's free hand at the end of the strapping of IV line. She stirred, mumbled, 'Mummy?' without opening her eyes, and resettled.

Raimondo closed his eyes. Then opened

them to stare up at Faith. 'And you have been alone through this.'

Faith nodded.

'She looks so pale.' He compressed his lips and gave her a rueful smile. 'I spoke to Finn. Your phone? He said it was dead, which was better than me thinking you had banned me from talking to you.'

She'd so wanted to talk to him. 'I wouldn't do that.'

He shrugged and squeezed her for a moment. 'How can I know that when I have wronged you again?'

'You did what you had to. And I had no charger. We left so quickly. One of the nurses is bringing me one from home tomorrow.'

'Of course.' He touched her hand. 'But I could not sit in the back of the taxi as I was being driven here from the airport and not find out what was happening. So I found Finn.' He shrugged apologetically.

She had to smile, though it felt so long since she had smiled her face felt stiff. 'I forgive you.'

'You will not need a phone to contact me for I will be here.'

'You're staying?'

'I have said I would never leave again.' His face was intense. 'Believe me.'

And looking at his strong, tired face, his warm eyes that searched to see if she was able to believe him, she did. 'Then I will. Now. With all my heart.'

He squeezed her to him. Then, even with that brief hug, she could feel the recharge of energy she'd stolen from him and straightened her shoulders. There was hope everywhere.

CHAPTER SIXTEEN

Isabel

ONE MONTH LATER, and two days before the wedding, Dominico Salvanelli, the groom's twin brother, stood by Isabel's side in the church as everyone practised for the wedding.

Isabel's hand rested on his admittedly very powerful forearm as they walked together back up the aisle, and she tried not to inhale the particularly divine aftershave he wore. Or glance across at his impressive chest that rose beside her so that she felt tiny.

Seriously, he was there every time she turned around, not saying anything. As if he was trying to understand something. Watching her. Which was ridiculous.

She wasn't one for toy boys and the man

was seven years her junior. Though, behind his eyes, she had the feeling he was decades older than her. These Salvanellis certainly knew how to do dark and mysterious.

Look at her niece's man. Though when she did, all she could see was joy. Which made Isabel smile.

Dominico leaned in to say something but paused as another instruction came from the priest. They turned and Dominico reluctantly let her go to return to the altar to stand beside his brother. They did it all again one more time.

'I think he likes you.' Faith was grinning at her as she did her stately bridal walk past, a particularly unfazed, calm bride. How come she, Isabel, the maid of honour, had all the nerves since Dominico had arrived?

Isabel whispered as she and Faith stood together to enter, 'He's too young. And he's got issues.'

Faith rolled her eyes at her. 'Issues are right up your alley.'

'You're being silly.' But she couldn't stop the heat creeping up her cheeks.

'I've never seen you blush before, Izzy,' Faith teased. 'Even when that locum doctor asked you out.'

The next few minutes were blessedly question-free until she was back down the aisle with Dominico's corded muscles beneath her arm again.

'It should be you who brings Chloe over to our villa while the honeymooners tour Italy and France.' Dominico's voice was low.

Isabel raised her brows. 'They will only be away two weeks.'

Dominico inclined his head. 'They could then stay longer.' He shrugged. 'For my new sister-in-law's peace of mind when her daughter is in Europe while she is away from Australian shores, of course.'

Isabel glanced sideways with mild amusement at him. 'And what would Chloe and I do while waiting in Florence?'

'There is much to see.' He lifted his head and smiled. Slowly and with a definitely wicked slant. Quite shocking after all the serious faces she'd seen from him earlier. 'I would show you both around, of course.'

Isabel laughed. 'Thank you for the invitation. We'll see what Faith wants to do.'

'Not what you wish?'

'I always do what I wish.'

Two days later

Raimondo's heart thumped with slow, vast joy at the front of the white church on the hill above the waves. He lifted his face to the light and with infinite patience, indeed he owed his bride that, and with his brother Dominico's shoulders level with his, they faced the round stained-glass depiction of Christ together and waited for Faith and her party to arrive.

To those seated on the pews, waiting with them for the ceremony to begin, they must look like two dark men in this place of light.

Beside him, Dominico's face seemed hewn like the painted granite of the church, inscrutable as he stared ahead in his matching black suit. Raimondo had no doubt his brother was remembering his own tragic marriage and the loss of his family.

He would not have gloom today. 'Brother?' Dominico turned to look at him and thankfully Raimondo noted the strain ease away. 'Today is for rejoicing, yes?'

'Indeed.' Dominico's mouth kinked upwards. 'I rejoice. You managed to wait a whole month before you married her.'

Raimondo laughed quietly. 'It was not

possible for more speed or it certainly would have been sooner. Thank you for being here.' It had been difficult to extricate his brother from the many technicalities of an incinerated business, and a lethargy steeped in despair, but even Dominico had known he would have to come if Raimondo married in Australia.

Raimondo smiled internally to himself as he stood, basking in the early afternoon sunshine through the round window, and waited with an eager heart for his beautiful bride. How much time he, Raimondo, had wasted without Faith by his side.

Faith and Chloe. How could a man be so fortunate? He would ensure that he earned it in his care of his wife and daughter for the rest of his life. Perhaps they would be blessed by more family as well.

He had to sympathise with his brother on the irresistible attraction of the Fetherstone women.

At the wedding rehearsal his brother had been unusually taken with the maid of honour, but Isabel had brushed off Dominico's attention as if she were the older, wiser woman fussed over by a boy. It had been amusing to Raimondo when she was only seven years the elder and Dominico… Well, his brother had been markedly ruffled by her dismissal.

His smile kicked at the thought but he knew better than to say anything.

Dominico had reluctantly left Florence with every intention of hurrying home as soon as the nuptials were completed. Though, to Raimondo's delight, it had taken just one evening in the company of Isabel Fetherstone for Dominico to mention to his brother that he might stay 'perhaps a little longer'.

After the honeymoon, he and Faith would return here to live, where the sea breeze blew salty whispers through the open windows of the houses along with the sound of crashing waves and circling gulls.

This bay, this place, held magic the like of which he had never seen before and watching his brother had made him pray for the healing of his sibling's heart as well.

He glanced over his shoulder to see in the congregation Faith's friends and colleagues who would be his associates when he began work here. Yes, he could live here very happily for the rest of his life. There would be many times when he flew home but never again would he leave his new family behind.

But that did not dim the expectation of showing Faith and Chloe his world. The delight of that was for the future.

A car pulled up. He heard the doors open and his heart rate picked up. Soon. Soon he would see the woman he would spend the rest of his life with.

The music started and a rustling at the door and shift of light drew all eyes to the entrance.

Raimondo strained to see his bride.

Ah. The little flower girls. His daughter, his Chloe like a daffodil in her sunshine-yellow dress, the lilac sash so pretty, her dark hair plaited around her sweet, serious face as she solemnly sprinkled yellow rose petals down the aisle for the bride. Little Piper followed her, her own basket of dewy softness on her arm as she copied her friend. They looked like fairies as their glowing faces spread joy like petals among the congregation.

Isabel stepped into view, head up, large eyes excited, yet her face serene, her mouth curved in the happiness of the moment, and

Raimondo felt his brother tense beside him. *Sì*, she was a vision. But not Raimondo's vision.

There Faith's aunt waited, the maid of honour who'd refused to be a bridesmaid, the pale lilac dress highlighting the dark auburn of her hair, the silk that slid and slithered over the slim body modestly but with that hint of allure he found abundantly in Faith. Isabel stepped sideways and the music lifted to a climax and there she was.

His bride. Standing in the doorway. Her inner light bathing him with love from fifty feet away as she caught and captured his gaze. His angel. His love. His Faith.

Dios. So beautiful. Glorious. In that moment he swore he would never fall short of her needs again as he stood drinking in the sight of her as she paused in her walk towards him. His swelling heart overflowed with gratitude for this woman, so beautiful inside and out, and the love she offered him made his heart swell.

Faith stopped at the entrance to the church as she reached out and rested her hand lightly on Isabel's arm. Isabel, her aunt, her friend, her rock, was the one to give her away for safekeeping into the arms of the man she loved, as she should be.

She'd never thought this time would come, her at the front of a church, Raimondo waiting at the end of the aisle with such a powerful love shining her way she almost lifted off the ground with it, so it was with surprise she realised her fingers didn't shake. That there was no caution as she threw herself and Chloe into this headlong rush of marriage.

No doubts since the hospital, no doubts since Raimondo had promised his inclusion fully in their future. No doubts since he'd returned to stay by her side.

Now she could imagine nothing else.

The time was here.

She looked ahead to where her husband-to-be seemed to fill the end of the aisle in his black tuxedo and white silk shirt, a yellow rose in his lapel, his eyes on her. Yes, his brother stood beside him but she had eyes only for Raimondo.

Their eyes held and now her belly twitched and came alive. Her heart rate sped up and her breathing increased.

Yes, Raimondo. I'm coming. She lifted her head and stepped forward, Isabel by her side, and closed the distance between herself and the man she would always love.

* * * * *

If you missed the previous stories in the Midwives of Lighthouse Bay trilogy, look out for

A Month to Marry the Midwife
Healed by the Midwife's Kiss

And if you enjoyed this story, check out these other great reads from Fiona McArthur

Midwife's Marriage Miracle
Midwife's Christmas Proposal
Midwife's Mistletoe Baby

All available now!